LISTEN TO ME,
GRACE KELLY

LISTEN TO ME, GRACE KELLY

Sandy Frances Duncan

KIDS CAN PRESS LTD.
Toronto

Kids Can Press Ltd. acknowledges with appreciation the assistance of the Canada Council and the Ontario Arts Council in the production of this book.

Canadian Cataloguing in Publication Data

Duncan, Frances, 1942-
    Listen to me, Grace Kelly

ISBN 1-55074-012-1

I. Title

PS8557.U537L58   1990   jC813'.54   C90-094339-4
Pz7.D86Li 1990

Kids Can Press Ltd.
585 ½ Bloor Street West,
Toronto, Ontario, Canada   M6G 1K5

Edited by Charis Wahl
Designed by N.R. Jackson
Typeset by Pixel Graphics Inc.
Printed and bound in Canada by Webcom Ltd.

90 0 9 8 7 6 5 4 3 2 1

For Ross and Tom and Jean
For Barrie, Blair and John, earlier
For George, later
For Susan

ACKNOWLEDGEMENTS

The author gratefully acknowledges
the kind help and interest of
Bessie Marshall and
Alice Nolan of Emsdale, Ontario.

This book was written with the aid of
grants from the Canada Council.

AUTHOR'S NOTES

Grace Kelly (1929-1982) appeared in ten movies before her engagement to Prince Rainier was announced on January 5, 1956. I have moved the announcement ahead six months. Oleg Cassini, a fashion designer, had been one of Grace Kelly's previous escorts.

The disease that Jess's father had was first described by Dr. Alois Alzheimer in 1906 and is correctly called Alzheimer's Disease. However, during the 1940s, 50s, and even the 60s, little was written or talked about this disease. Consequently, in 1955, Jess would have been told that her father suffered from arteriosclerosis (hardening of the arteries of the brain) or pre-senile dementia. Neither of these terms is now used for this disease process.

CHAPTER

ONE

Sometimes my stomach tickles and I hear a buzz like a thousand bees. That's my signal something important is happening. I had it for one whole day a year ago and that night Mum said we were moving to Toronto. But sometimes I get the signal and then it stops and nothing has happened. I used to worry about that, but not any more. Something may have happened and I just don't know what.

I felt buzzy and tickly almost the minute we got here so I know I have to remember every detail of this summer. Something will be significant. Suppose I become a famous movie star like Grace Kelly and someone interviews me fifty years from now on radio or TV—someone like Ed Sullivan waving his arms and running his hand over his hair the way he does while everyone claps—

We have a really big SHEW for you tonight starring—Jessica Crawford! I bow to thunderous applause. Now, Jessica—Ed Sullivan grabs my arm above the elbow—it is obvious that of all the things that have happened in your glamorous and star-studded life, the summer of 1955 contained the most important. Think back and tell our viewing audience what you remember—

What if I can't remember a thing? Of course, then I could really be like Grace Kelly and refuse to comment—It's no one's business what I wear to sleep in—

Still, I'd rather be able to remember. Not that anything has happened yet. That I know of.

We just arrived at Lake of Bays yesterday, Saturday, Agatha Adams, Mum and me. This evening Mum'll go back to Toronto till Friday night, so there'll only be Agatha and me. Agatha is the first grown-up I've ever called just—Agatha. She is seventy-five. I am twelve and a half. At seventy-five you don't count halves. Seventy-five is old.

A couple of months ago, Mum hung up the phone laughing and shaking her head. "That was Agatha scolding me for not phoning her all week."

Mum mimicked, " 'Eleanor, I'm an old lady, I might be dead for all you know!' " Mum made it the joke of the week, told her bridge friends and they laughed too, but I didn't think it was funny.

I hope Agatha doesn't die this summer. I hope that's not why I have the signal. What would I do?

This is a neat place, the cottage with trees all around and the lake coming right up to my cave here—I couldn't wait to get out of the car, four hours from Toronto. I was squished in the back with the clothes and food and pillows, though I didn't mind that. I stared out the window and pretended I was riding a horse along the grassy edge of the road. I can pretend so well I can feel the horse. Sometimes we canter, sometimes we slow to a walk, and other times we jump ditches or big rocks. Still, four hours is a long time on horseback, especially if you can't move around because of the boxes and pillows. So when Agatha said, "Turn here, Eleanor" and Mum said, "Where?" and Agatha said, "Back there" and Mum reversed and found the overgrown opening in the trees and a post with a sign that might have said *Adams* once and bumped down a dirt road and stopped the Studebaker in a small grassy clearing, I couldn't wait to get out.

The sun-hot grass smelled up at me thick with clover and tall white flowers, and then the moist

3

path overhung with branches. I didn't know what I wanted to explore first, the cottage or the lake. I wanted to run to both at once, like reading the first pages of two library books before burying yourself in one, but Mum shouted, "Take something with you!" I grabbed a couple of pillows and ran down the path.

The cottage surprised me, looming up, dark and very old and weathered, the same brown as the ground. A path led to an outhouse hidden in the trees. I dropped the pillows on the back stoop and followed the stone base of the cottage around to the front. A screened veranda the whole length of it. Dried grass and dandelions in the rust-coloured sand—then the lake, a brilliant blue with white birches growing right down to the water, and, not far out, a small rocky island with two trees.

I stood there with my hands in my pockets, looking from cottage to lake and back again. Not what I'd expected. Not a green squatter's shack on a rocky ocean beach like the one we had at Dollarton.

Dummy, I said to myself. You should have known. Nothing in Ontario is like Vancouver. They don't even speak the same, rad for radiator, ex for exhibition, thought I was from England, said *I* had the accent. And fireworks on May

4

twenty-fourth instead of Hallowe'en. This cottage is a two-storey house as big as some in the city. This lake has no tide, no seaweed smell, no barnacly rocks.

Well, you knew it wouldn't have, Jess.

I guess I didn't know what it would have.

When I don't know what to expect, I fill the *what* with the closest thing I do know. And that's when my stomach began to tickle and I heard the buzz like a thousand bees.

I walked back to the cottage. Mum was shaking the pillows I'd dropped on the stoop. She gave me her exasperated look.

Inside is an enormous room with a floor-to-ceiling fireplace made of the same round stones as the outside foundation. A kitchen counter with a tin sink and a pump along the back wall. A wood cookstove in the corner. Except for the pump and the fireplace, those are the same as the Dollarton shack. So are the heavy shutters Mum and I struggled off the windows. Light came in and showed a long wooden table with two chairs on each side facing one another and, in front of the fireplace, comfortable lumpy chairs covered in faded blue flowers, perfect for reading. A bookcase stuffed with paperbacks. Pictures on the walls I could look at later, a door to a bedroom, and wide stairs against the far wall. Tucked in

5

behind the staircase was a rollaway cot I could put on the veranda.

Proper cottage furniture. I grinned with relief. My complete mental picture of Lake of Bays had had our small shack at Dollarton crammed full of Agatha's Toronto apartment furniture: red velvet Victorian chairs, a sofa with carved wooden pieces that dig in everywhere I try to get comfortable, and dusty-looking African violets holding doilies down on teetery, spindly tables.

I walked over to the sink and lifted the handle of the pump. The cool metal resisted. I pulled harder. A sucking whine as the handle came up. Pushed down. A loud clatter. I did it again, again.

"You have to prime it," said Agatha. I glanced at her, puzzled.

"With water from the lake," Mum explained. "Otherwise it just sucks air."

"Forever?" I was still pumping. Wheeze. Clatter.

"Not forever. It will break first." Agatha's sandpaper tone.

"Oh." Carefully I returned the handle to its resting position. We didn't have a pump at Dollarton. We carried water from the spring or the gas station on the road.

"I've always slept upstairs," Agatha was saying,

"but I'll take the downstairs room this summer, just in case—"

"In case what?" I asked.

"In case you need looking after. I'm not getting any younger." Her mouth down-turned, was she glaring? I clenched my teeth—just how old does she think I am?

"None of us are." Mum laughed her soothing laugh and gave me her don't-say-anything look. "Jess won't need looking after, Agatha. She's pretty independent. Still—it's a good idea for you to sleep on this floor."

Agatha nodded at me as if satisfied, and I tried to smile. Mum's a social worker, maybe that's why she can stop fights and keep everyone happy. Not that I'd have fought with Agatha. She *is* seventy-five and I've been told often enough to respect my elders. Stand up when they enter the room, pass them the sandwiches first—

"Jessica can sleep upstairs in my old room," Agatha continued. She had both hands on her cane, stiff-armed, as if she'd rather swing it than lean on it.

"I'd like to sleep outside—on the veranda." I looked at Mum and crossed my fingers.

Agatha snapped, "It's cold at night. The screening's old. Mosquitoes get in."

7

Mum unlocked the front door and stepped out. I started after her, remembered. Backing up politely, I let Agatha go ahead. A huge veranda open on three sides to the lake and trees and sky. I couldn't see any holes in the screening. Mum said, "Oh, how lovely. Much bigger than the porch on the shack."

"I used to sleep out there all the time," I offered. "And Scott and Pete, my friends next door, we slept out at home. We pinned blankets to the edges of our huge beach umbrella to make a tent—"

Mum asked, "Did you ever sleep out as a child, Agatha?"

Agatha rubbed the palm of her hand on her cane and inspected the pale green walls, posts, veranda ceiling. A fuzzy grey spider's nest glued in a corner near the outside door. "Gracious, no! I didn't have this screened until after the war—"

Agatha looked towards the lake, looked farther away than the lake. "My brother and I tried to once. I must have been eight or nine or Jess's age. We took bedding to the arbour in our garden. But our mother found us and we had to stay inside for a week in case we might come down with the grippe." She sort of smiled. At least, her lip twitched. "I'd forgotten that."

"Like Scott and Pete and me—but our mothers

let us," I added, trying to imagine her mother. Agatha blinked at me, startled, then nodded.

"So I'll sleep upstairs in your old room," said Mum.

Then Mum and I unloaded the Studebaker and Agatha put the food in the cupboards. On one trip Mum whispered, "I think Agatha doesn't want to go up and down the stairs to a bedroom in case she falls, but she's too proud to admit that."

"Oh!" So she didn't think I was a baby after all! But I do wish people would say what they mean. It's so confusing when they don't.

CHAPTER

TWO

We unpacked and put things away. I made up the
cot on the veranda, then brought a pail of water
from the lake and poured it into the pump. Mum
had greased around the handle. I pulled, pushed.
It still clattered, but didn't wheeze. Trickle—gush,
gush. Water slopped into the sink and splashed
onto the counter. Like making my own waterfall.
Once I'd dammed a little creek behind our house
in Vancouver, and when it had grown to a pond
and was fingering other ways around the rocks, I
pulled them out. Water had roared and foamed
until finally it subsided to its previous trickle.
Now I pumped and pumped, wanting to see how
fast this water could pour in. But Mum put her

hand on mine, frowning. "You'll have it worked off the counter, Jess. The bolts are worn." I guess I'd got carried away. It's hard to stop pumping once you start.

I went exploring, and that's when I found my cave. Well—half a cave. But right at the edge of the lake. The bank is high on two sides and the trees overhang the water as if each branch wants a drink. Earth has fallen away so the tree roots are bare. I moved some rocks and brushed the loose dirt with my hands. I lay between two big comfortable roots and looked at the lake lapping right at my feet, the water speckled dark or glinting as the branches moved. I could almost pretend it was the ocean, except there was no tide line, just a scurf of sand and fallen leaves—a no-tide line.

I ran up to the cottage for a pillow. Outside the door, I looked back to check and saw only the bank of earth and thick branches. Perfectly private. When I lay down in my cave again with my head on the pillow, I could see sky like puzzle pieces through sun-backed, lime-green leaves, a white birch trunk and lake with a bit of the island. A bird chirped nearby. Happiness filled me and I drummed my fingers on the dirt.

All my life I've found private places outdoors. At Dollarton, I had a branch of a large cedar tree.

No one ever thought to look up for me. At home, I crawled between two droopy rhododendrons in the corner of the backyard. I'd escaped there a lot when my father was sick. But I've never had a cave. I can read here or think. I won't tell Agatha or Mum. I won't even show it to Lynn when she comes for a week.

Suppose Grace Kelly were staying at that lodge I can see a bit of across the lake—Bigwin Inn, Agatha said, the round part's the boathouse—and her boat got into trouble and I swam out and rescued her. I'd show her this place.

What a wonderful cave, Jessica. It's so private.

Thank you. Step down here carefully, Grace Kelly, you don't want to get your white gloves dirty.

That's all right, they're an old pair.

Let me say, Grace Kelly, how much I admire your acting. I especially like *Rear Window* and *To Catch a Thief*. I read every article I find about you in the movie magazines.

How kind of you, Jessica. I'm honoured to have such a devoted fan. Why don't you fly back to Hollywood with me and I'll show you around the studio? You can stay with me.

Thank you for the invitation. I'll ask my mother, but I don't suppose it's possible this summer. I'm looking after Agatha. Why don't you stay here with me?

I'm sorry, I can't. I have to make another movie. My career keeps me so busy. But let's write each other—we can be best friends.

Oh, Grace Kelly! Do you really want me for a best friend?

Of course.

But I'm best friends with Lynn.

You can have two best friends. Lynn won't mind.

You're sure you want me? You're so regal and sophisticated, so—perfect.

No one's perfect, Jessica.

Maybe not, Grace Kelly, but if anyone is, you are. Even your hair's always perfect.

Don't forget, I have a hair dresser at the movie studio.

Well—you look like nothing bad's ever happened to you.

I try. Now tell me, Jessica, who is Agatha?

Well, Grace Kelly, it's like this—are you comfortable there? Would you like another cushion? I'd hate for you to get dirt on that pretty dress.

She laughs—my dresses never get dirty.

You're so lucky. Mine always do, that's why I wear jeans or shorts most of the time. I bet you don't sweat either, do you? Perspire, I mean. Mum says, "Horses sweat, men perspire, ladies shed little drops of dew." You're a real lady, Grace Kelly. Not like Marilyn Monroe. She looks like she sweats. I don't go to her movies at all, though Lynn says she's okay, she has sex appeal like Elvis. I don't like him, either. I only like you. But I don't think I'll ever be a lady. I get dirty. And I sweat. Like a horse.

There, there. She smiles. You do talk a lot, don't you?

Only to you, Grace Kelly! Do you mind? I can be quiet. Very quiet. I've had lots of practice.

No, no, it's fine. I wasn't criticizing.

But her tone was critical. I roll the edge of my shorts between my thumb and finger and watch an ant searching in the dirt. She touches my shoulder and I look up, into her understanding blue eyes. At her delicately lipsticked mouth, her whole beautiful face, her perfect pageboy. She didn't mean to criticize. I smile.

Now about Agatha—

Oh, yes. Agatha is a friend of my father's family from when they lived in Toronto before the First World War—

What a long time ago!

Yes—anyway, when we moved to Toronto last year, Mum remembered Agatha had written her

14

after the funeral. But Mum had lost her address so she started calling all the Adams in the phonebook. Good thing Agatha's an A or Mum'd be phoning still. Do you know how many Adams there are? Pages.

Probably as many as Kelly.

No, more. I checked. I think about you a lot, you know. I want to be like you. I wish you lived with me.

I'm touched. She reaches out and pats my knee.

Anyway, when Agatha said in the spring how much she wanted to spend the summer at her cottage—it might be her last summer, she said—but couldn't do it alone, Mum said we'd come along. Except Mum has to work so she can only be here weekends until her holidays—

Aren't you going to be lonely? Just you and an old lady?

I don't think so. I can always talk to you—if you don't mind? Grace Kelly smiles and shakes her head. And Agatha says there's a stable a few miles down the road and a bus that goes there so I can ride, and there're lots of books, and my friend Lynn's coming to stay for a week, and there's the whole lake to swim in and I can find out things from Agatha about my father—

What sort of things?

Oh—what he was like before—

Where is your father?

Oh, he died when I was eight.

That's so sad.

I'm not sad. I can show you a picture of him all dressed up in his kilt and medals. He was really handsome and he was a war hero. Agatha knew him then. That was before Mum married him. Hey, you've never made a war movie! You could make one about him! Gary Cooper could be my father!

Then I'd be your mother.

Oh. (Mum wouldn't like that. I felt curdled with disloyalty.)

Grace Kelly and I laugh. I bet you're a good actress, Jessica. I duck my head and blush. Her tone changes. I'm close to my father. I'd hate it if he died.

Maybe you would, Grace Kelly, most people would, but I'm not most people. I don't mind. And I know you have a big family, but in mine there's just Mum and me.

An only child and no father, that's dreadful. You must be spoiled.

Oh! Some best friend! Are you like Lynn and everyone else thinking an only child must be spoiled or lonely? Mum doesn't spoil me and I'm not lonely! And I'm not sad my father's dead! I

16

think your boat's fixed now, Grace Kelly. Why don't you go back to Bigwin Inn?

She wouldn't really have said that, I thought, if she knew Mum. Besides, I yelled after her, I have lots of relatives and friends in Vancouver!

CHAPTER

THREE

After dinner I carried Mum's overnight bag up the trail to the car. "I wish you didn't have to leave." I opened the driver's door and flung the bag onto the front seat.

"So do I." Mum gave me a hug. "But I do, so let's make the best of it."

I leaned my head on her shoulder. "I wish you didn't have to work." Mum squeezed me harder, patted my back. "I wish you'd win the Irish Sweepstakes so you wouldn't have to work."

Mum laughed. "So do I, Jess. Well, maybe the next Sweepstakes. But you know, if wishes—"

"—were horses, beggars would ride," I finished with her. "I know."

I wanted to say I wish I could come with you or I wish I could have gone home to Vancouver for the summer, but I couldn't. Mum might get her look. I knew she thought Agatha and Lake of Bays a really good solution for my holidays. Right now I could think of a million things I'd rather do. Go to a camp where teenagers blow whistles and give you orders. Wander around Toronto all by myself in the heat. Sit in my bedroom and never come out.

I looked up. Mum was smiling at me. She gave me a last squeeze and kiss and climbed into the car. "It's not long until Friday." I didn't agree, but I said nothing. "You have a good time," Mum continued, "and—well, I don't have to tell you to be good and help Agatha." She rolled down the window, then slammed the door.

"What if she dies?" I blurted.

Mum laughed and reached through the window for my hand. "That's highly unlikely, Jess!"

"She's older than my father was!"

Mum turned her head so I wouldn't see her frowning at the windshield. She sighed. My hand felt hot and limp in hers. I wished I'd kept my mouth shut. Any time I mention my father, she frowns and sighs. I hate making her do that—get her look.

Mum turned back. She had on a little smile,

but her eyes were still frowning. "Agatha's in excellent health, Jess, except for her arthritis. She'll probably live for years. Don't you worry." She squeezed my hand. "Now give me a kiss, I have to get going. And promise you won't worry."

"I'll try not to," was the best I could mutter, but she looked satisfied. I kissed her cheek, then backed away as she started the car.

I waved until I couldn't see her any longer. I listened until I couldn't hear the car any longer. Silence and heat hung heavy in the clearing. I tried to cross it without stepping on any tree shadows, like not stepping on sidewalk cracks. But the trail on the other side was totally shaded.

"Hello," I said, opening the back door.

Agatha looked up from the dishes she was washing. "Hello, Jessica." She continued looking at me looking at her. I wished Lynn were here right now, not two weeks from now. She'd know what to say. She can talk to anybody, even strangers on the street, even boys.

"Would you like me to finish the dishes for you?" I still had my hand on the doorknob.

"No, thank you, Jessica. I like washing up." She was looking at me as if I were a stranger she had to memorize. Agatha is dumpy and stoop-shouldered with long white hair that wisps out of her bun, a large nose, and four bristles on her

20

chin. If I'd been younger than eleven when I met her, I'd have thought she looked like the witch with the poisoned apple in Snow White. Even though we've seen her maybe once a month since we moved to Toronto last August, this is the first time she and I have been alone together.

"Would you like me to dry?"

"No, thank you."

She was still looking at me. I stood straighter, then had to scratch my knee. All of me was getting itchy. I cleared my throat. "Is anything wrong?"

Agatha blinked, fished a soapy fork out of the dishpan. "No." Still looking. "Actually, I was thinking how much you look like your father when he was young. I hadn't noticed it before."

"Really?" I shivered, though I wasn't cold. "But he had blond hair."

"His sister, Mary, had your brown."

"Poor thing," I said sincerely.

"Not at all! She had lovely hair! You have the family resemblance around the eyes and chin."

"Oh." I was smiling. If that was what Agatha was thinking, she could keep on looking forever. But she put the fork on the drainboard and pulled out a plate. "Mum's side of the family say I look like *her*," I offered, hoping she'd continue.

But Agatha shrugged. "It was perhaps only a

momentary resemblance, Jessica. Best to look like yourself."

"What did he look like?"

"Surely you've seen photos?"

"Yes, but—" Old photos that have faded to brown and beige. They could be pictures of any man with a pipe and a hat or a uniform.

"He looked like those then." Agatha turned all her attention back to the dishes. I was just about to ask her what he was like when she said, "Why don't you go off and play?"

Play! No one's told me to play in years! Not since my father was sick. Everyone told me to go and play then. Just to get rid of me, I knew that, even then. My chest started to hurt. My eyes felt gritty. I wished Mum hadn't left or I'd gone with her or Lynn were here. Nobody'd tell Lynn to play!

"If you don't need me, I think I'll read a book," I said in my most dignified tone. It was shaping up to be a long summer. As long as those other summers, before he died? But still, I looked like him, even a bit?

CHAPTER

FOUR

Every day after Agatha washes the lunch dishes, she goes to her room for her afternoon "read." Within minutes her snoring almost rattles the door. I guess you could call it "reading" aloud. I've been lying on my bed on the veranda reading too, most of the time since Mum left, listening to the bash of bugs on the screen punctuate Agatha's snores, but each day has been hotter. By Wednesday even the effort of lying still made me sweat. I just couldn't put off swimming any longer.

I pulled on my bathing suit, draped a towel around my neck and collected the carton of salt I'd brought from Toronto. Ever since I was three when I jumped off a wharf into water over my head and my father pulled me out, I've been swimming. In the summers before we moved to Toronto, Mum would come home from work and take me and Scott and Pete, my best home friends, to the beach. And I always swam at Dollarton. At highest tide, the water came right under the pilings of the shack and I could jump in off the porch. But that was the ocean.

When I told the kids at school Mum and I were moving to Toronto, Barbara said lakes have big brown slimy leeches that stick to your skin and suck your blood out and you can only get them off with salt. Barbara lived here. She should know.

My teacher said I'd love "the autumnal colours of Ontario trees," and that was sure true last fall. It almost made up for no fireworks on Hallowe'en. At home the leaves only rust a bit at the edges then get rained off the branches and turn to mush in the gutters, but here they change into crimson, scarlet, orange, yellow—like a postcard made real—and stay that way for weeks. I couldn't get enough of looking at them, even though I thought they were a bit show-offy.

Leaves were true, so leeches must be. I've worried for weeks. Just thinking about them makes my goose-bumps crawl. How can I swim without being attacked? Yet there's that island—

I've never had an island to swim to. In the ocean all I had to worry about were barnacles and kelp strands, jellyfish and rip-tides.

I put my salt carton right at the edge of the lake and my towel beside it and squatted down to examine the water. My reflection, slightly rippled—wish my hair would hold a pageboy like Grace Kelly's, wish it were blond, even my father's was blond, wish I had her sort of nose, mine doesn't fit—below, a few bright green, grassy weeds, a sort of dirt-sand bottom, and the occasional small stone. No leeches.

I put my index finger in as far as the first knuckle and stirred the water—maybe you have to hold still to be attacked, maybe if I swim very fast—

Lots of people grow up swimming in lakes and they survive. I did.

Yes, Grace Kelly.

Agatha has swum in this lake, and you know if she thought leeches were a problem she would have told you.

Yes, Grace Kelly. But Barbara said—

Barbara's a scaredy-cat. Remember how silly she was about the ocean, afraid a shark might eat her?

Yes, Grace Kelly. But maybe that was because she knew about leeches.

Jessica, I am disappointed in you. If I were there and wanted to swim, you wouldn't let leeches stop your joining me.

No, Grace Kelly.

So get in that water. You have your salt.

I stood up and put a foot in. The mud-sand squished between my toes. Not rocks or hard sand like the ocean. I waded out to my knees and belly-flopped into a breast-stroke so I wouldn't have to touch bottom. The water felt fresh-water funny. No salt to sting my eyes. I rolled over and floated, staying close to shore just in case, the trees bright green against the sky, moss on the roof of the cottage, the chimney looking tilted from here, and my cave a dark hollow.

When I was very small, before my father got sick, he and Mum and I had picnic suppers on the city beaches. We have a photo of me and him building a sand castle—at least that's what Mum says it was. She must have taken the picture. Just looks like a pile of sand to me, with a paper napkin flag on its highest lump. I was so small I only wore bathing-suit bottoms. He was wearing a shirt and trousers—Mum says he sunburned, because of his blond complexion. Wish I remembered. Maybe he and I dug a trench to the water and watched the tide inch up to fill the moat. That's what I used to do at the beach. Maybe he carried me on his shoulders back to Mum sitting by a log—oh yeah, he did, so high up I was scared and held onto his hat—it fell off, I grabbed his hair, I was falling—

AAAH! Something tickling me!

I leapt right up and splashed my way to shore—ugh! ugh! ugh!—stubbed my toe and fell down, grabbed my salt and pried at the opening. I couldn't bear to look at my leg, tickling everywhere, I knew I had a thousand leeches sucking my blood out, ugh, vampires! The salt wouldn't open, my leg was stinging, I could feel the blood dripping down, soon I wouldn't have any blood left, my throat gagged closed, going to throw up. Shivering and starting to sob, so scared, bent my fingernail prying at the spout—there.

Without looking, I twisted around and let the salt gush out all over the back of my leg. I could feel the leeches dropping off, I was panting against the hard beat of my heart.

Slowly, very slowly, I opened my eyes and looked at the ground, expecting to see millions of slimy brown things writhing their death throes. I looked behind me, looked at my leg, examined my other leg. No leeches. A lot of salt. Trickling white down my leg, piled on the ground. Though maybe leeches shrivel into nothing the minute salt touches them, maybe they become invisible, maybe they turn into salt themselves, maybe their corpses are buried under the little piles around my foot, maybe—No leeches. I suddenly felt very silly. I was glad Grace Kelly wasn't here. I suppose a piece of weed touched my leg.

Sometimes, Jess, you let your imagination run away with you.

Yes, Mum, I replied, and shook the salt carton. Empty. Oh well, there's some in the cottage. And we can buy more on the weekend.

I dove into the water and swam my fastest crawl to the island, pulled myself up and looked at my arms and legs. No leeches. I lay on the sun-hot rock and thought about how I'd never liked Barbara anyway, whiny, lying, stuck-up snob. Maybe the only leeches in the world are in Equatorial Africa.

If Scott and Pete were here, they'd want to find a leech. To see what it looks like. To put salt on it—like we did to a slug. Ugh, long, slimy grey-green thing. Its juices oozed out in the salt. Scott and Pete felt sorry then, but I couldn't look. I should have told Barbara slugs are much worse than leeches, they're bigger and slimier—but they don't suck blood. The only bad thing about slugs is stepping on them—or looking at them. I haven't seen any slugs in Ontario—yet.

A blue dragonfly lit on my knee and I shooed it

28

off. A horsefly buzzed around my head—around and around. I waved my arm but it only widened its flight path, then closed in again when I lay still. Finally it won; I dove into the water.

When I swam back, Agatha had finished her afternoon "read" and was standing at the shore, holding the empty salt carton. She asked, "Where did this come from?"

"It's mine."

"Is lake water not good enough for you? Do you want to recreate the ocean?" Her tone was sharp, but she was smiling. I'm getting a bit used to Agatha. Though not to the way her false teeth don't fit so she sometimes whistles her s's.

"Leeches," I said.

"Oh, of course. You never can tell." She looked across the lake. "S(whistle)ome years there are and s(whistle)ome years there aren't."

I scuffed a pile of salt with my toe, dragged a trail to the water and watched it dissolve. Maybe Barbara hadn't lied. I guess I'll just have to put up with it—but I sure hope this is one of the aren't years.

CHAPTER

FIVE

Somehow Agatha and I have divided up the chores without even talking about them. She sweeps the floor—at least three times a day—washes the dishes (I pump the water) and cooks—which is good because all I can make is oatmeal porridge and salt-water taffy. I chop the kindling, clean the coal-oil-lamp chimneys and sprinkle lye down the outhouse hole.

Seems to me I've been sprinkling lye down outhouse holes all my life. It was my job at the Dollarton shack, and when I was ten I went to a camp where we took turns doing it. So I've developed a method. What you do is: as you walk up the trail, you unroll the top of the bag—being careful not to breathe on it or the fine white powder jumps into your nose and eyes—so you're ready when you reach the outhouse. Then you take a very deep breath and hold it. Now open the door, lift up the lid—if there is one over the hole—turn the bag upside down, hold on tight so the bag doesn't fall in (that happened to me once and I know Agatha wouldn't think it's funny), shake it about three times, bang the lid down and back out, then slam the door before you take another breath. I bet Grace Kelly doesn't know how fast you have to be to sprinkle lye in an outhouse while you're holding your breath.

The job I like best is chopping kindling. It's so satisfying the way the wood splits instantly if you hit it just right. I think it's a job Agatha liked too. I think she wishes she could still do it—though I don't know why she can't, it's pretty easy.

The first day she seemed doubtful I could manage even though I told her I'd chopped lots of wood—I even had my own hatchet at Dollarton—but still she came out to watch me. I held the wood carefully and hit it with the axe, pulled the axe out and hit it again.

Agatha said, "There's a safer way. Let me show you." She gave the wood a light tap so the axe bit, but instead of pulling the axe out she lifted it with the wood still attached and banged the whole

31

thing hard on the chopping block. The kindling splintered beautifully. She's right, and it's not just safer, it's easier.

She watched me split six more pieces. I began to get nervous and wished she'd go sweep the floor or have her afternoon read. I was about to say, "Why are you watching me—don't you think I can do it?" when I glanced at her face. It was sad and longing, and made me think of *National Geographic* pictures: old-looking starving children. So I didn't say anything, just picked up another piece and split that into four. She could watch me forever, I didn't care.

I don't think she was remembering splitting wood when she was my age. She's told me how well-brought-up she was, and back in the stone age well-brought-up girls didn't chop wood. They did needlework and wore gloves to a school that taught something called deportment. I think I'm well-brought-up too, even if I can chop wood. I own a pair of white gloves, and I know at tea parties you introduce the man to the lady and the younger person to the older person. Of course it's tricky deciding who's younger when they all have grey hair and remembering which way to do it— to say nothing of remembering their names. I usually help in the kitchen until that part is over.

I wonder where my white gloves are. I haven't

seen them in months. Does Grace Kelly ever lose hers?

We used to have furniture like Agatha's, too—all polished wood and velvet and heavy drapes I hid behind. Even an antique harpsichord. Mum played it sometimes. But we sold the furniture when we sold the house. Now we have rollaway cots and a second-hand chesterfield in our apartment. And plastic curtains. Though they're crinkly with bright flowers so they don't look plastic. It's much cheaper, Mum says.

I would have asked Agatha what she was thinking as she watched me split kindling, but she looked as if she might cry. I'd hate to have her cry. Anyway, I don't like being asked what I'm thinking, especially if I'm thinking about Grace Kelly. So I just smiled at her, but she was looking through me, not at me, as Mum says.

I couldn't get her look out of my mind though, and after dinner I curled up in one of the armchairs and asked, "What was it like here when you were my age, Agatha?"

Agatha slowed her rocking chair and turned to look at me. She was wearing a green and yellow flowered housedress that buttoned up the front and thick lisle stockings, even in this heat. I haven't seen her without stockings all week.

"This was one of the first cottages on Lake of

Bays, but before my father had it built, we holidayed at Port Cunnington Lodge up the lake. In those days we had to take the train from Union Station to Huntsville, stay overnight in the hotel, then drive out with horses and carriage. I was older than you are. We didn't start coming here until the turn of the century."

I subtracted fifty-five from seventy-five—Agatha would have been twenty in 1900. It was in 1892 that she was twelve like me. My father was born in 1887—he would have been five when Agatha was twelve. The eighteen-hundreds are so long ago. It's hard to believe people really lived then. If Mum had married my father earlier, I'd be grown up now. Grown up when he died maybe. But she couldn't have because he was in the war. Mum says the war mixed up the generations because so many men were killed. I wonder what Agatha did in the war.

Agatha seemed to be somewhere else, silently rocking through her memories. I'm not good at knowing what to say to keep people talking, not like Mum, so I looked at Agatha and thought, what's it like to be old?

Old is slow, I know that, and old is sleepy, and old is fussy. Agatha always sweeps the floor from the back door through the kitchen to the veranda, then has to bend over—which she doesn't do

34

well—to brush the dirt into the dustpan. I told her to start on the veranda and work the other way so she could sweep the dirt out the back door. She glared at me and said that was messy and not to teach my grandmother to suck eggs. Which I think is a disgusting expression—suck raw eggs? Next day I offered to hold the dustpan for her, but she said in a tight tone that she could manage. I figure she wants to do it her way.

Is old missing being young? Is old wishing you'd lived differently? Does Agatha wish she'd married and had children? Is she lonely? Does she think about death? Did my father? He was sixty-three when he died, that's old, but nowhere near as old as seventy-five—

I startled when Agatha cleared her throat. "I was engaged to be married when my father had this cottage built. He did it to please my mother, but he forgot to ask if it would please her. It didn't. She had to organize the household to change residences—the cook, maids, the gardener, who would stay in town and who would come here, who would pack the trunks and plan the food. She was city-bred and comfortable there and so, as it turned out, was my father. His pioneer spirit was more of a ghost." She smiled at her joke.

"What happened to your fiancé?" I was feeling

a thrill of shock that she'd ever been engaged, ever been in—love.

"He went off to fight in the Boer War like a good son of the Empire and got himself killed."

"Oh, I'm sorry! What a tragedy!" I clutched the arms of my chair.

She glared at me. "Don't waste your tears. It happened over fifty years ago!"

"That makes it even more sad and romantic." I could see him, handsome in his uniform, waving to a young, beautiful Grace Kelly-blond Agatha in a white dress, daintily dabbing her eyes with a hankie. "What war?" I asked. "And what was his name?"

"Jeremy. The Boer War in South Africa against the Dutch."

"Oh, you mean the Boor War! I thought you meant the war was boring!" I stopped myself laughing just in time.

But she was saying, "Pronunciation is a major problem nowadays. Bore—B O E R. The Dutch people were the Boers." She was shaking her head.

I said, "Jeremy's such a romantic name. Were you madly in love?"

Her face softened and was maybe smiling. "Jeremy was not an uncommon name then, but, yes, I too thought it romantic, and yes, I suppose I was in love, whatever that state is." She started to rock again, but I didn't want her to go back there silently.

"When you recovered from the tragedy, did you ever love another man?"

"No."

"How romantic! One great love and you never recovered!"

Agatha sniffed. "Actually, Jessica I took a good look around and decided marriage wasn't for me. The wives were all too confined—and not just by confinements—" Her lips curled in a cold smile. I'm realizing Agatha likes making jokes only she appreciates. "—even those with luxuries. I decided to follow the fine tradition of spinsterhood. When my mother convinced my father that the rural life did not suit them, I took over this cottage and I've been coming here every May and staying until September for fifty-three years. And during those years I've been—minding—my—own— business!" She separated those words with firm rocks of her chair, and I got the message.

The sun and birch trees were conspiring to send evening shadows into the cottage. June bugs and horseflies, slavering after the chicken we'd had for dinner, clanked against the screens.

Mosquitoes that made it through hummed and hovered and lit. I hit one on my leg—a smear of blood.

Suppose Jeremy hadn't been killed in the Boer War and had gone off to the First World War. He might have known my father. Maybe the man my father saved to get the medal for bravery would have been Jeremy.

Thank you for saving my life, Robert Crawford.

Not at all, Jeremy. It was no trouble. I just had to climb out of the trench and run over No Man's Land under German bullets and through poisonous gas and pull you back to safety.

I will be eternally grateful, Robert.

Nonsense, Jeremy. You would have done the same for me, had I been so dumb as to go out there in the first place.

You're right, Robert, it was dumb. I should have waited until we were all ready to attack and not tried to be a hero. That's what happened in the Boer War and I didn't have you to save me.

Both of them marching side by side down a street of cheering people, their kilts swinging to the bagpipe music like Armistice Day parades before my father got sick. When I was small, I helped him polish his boots and whiten his spats—tartan socks to his knees—the almost hidden skean-dhu, its cairngorm peering out at me like a scary yellow eye, his blond leg hairs curling over it like eyelashes, and way, way, way up above, his stern, unsmiling face—Cairngorm. Skean-Dhu. Kilt. Tartan. Sporran. Medals. Revolver. Sword. His old words broke into my mind. I was clutching the arms of the chair, holding my breath. I let it out very quietly.

"Agatha, what was—" I finished the sentence in my head "—my father like when you knew him?" Agatha was asleep, her mouth open, about to snore. Oh well, we are here for the rest of July and all of August.

CHAPTER

SIX

A giant is stalking across the grass. He sways from side to side with each stride, thump, thump, closer, closer, closer. He's huge as a building, dark clothes and a red, twisted face. Drool spatters from his lips. I don't want to watch but I'm frozen, looking through the living-room window. He's crossing the front lawn, he has a cane. Nowhere for me to hide. I can't run, my legs won't move. He's coming up the walk, thump, thump, up the steps. He's got leeches clinging to his head, long brown swollen leeches waving like wind-blown hair. They're falling down his face, dropping onto his shoulders. He's at the front door. He raises his stick to bang, thump, thump, thump, let me in! There's no one home but me. I slide behind the drape. Please, Mr. Giant, take my teddy bear, but don't hurt me!

Thump, ka-bang—he pushes the door open—he's in the house. My heart's beating everywhere. It's the whole room. He'll hear. I don't want to scream, he'll hear, he'll find me—oh please, Mr. Giant, go away. Can't help it, the scream's building in my throat, he's going to find me. I pull the drape tight around me, press into the wall—he's found me, he's poking through the drape with his stick—I've got my eyes closed tight but still I can see a leech—

I feel the fabric in my clenched fists, hurting so much they start to loosen. I try to hold on, but I can't. Roughness—a blanket? I'm hiding in a blanket then? My eyes open like my hands, pitch dark—he's holding me to him, blocking out the light—

But I can breathe. I can turn my head. Nothing over my face—

Stars. Shining through the veranda screen. My fingers still clutched the blanket as if it were drapery. I couldn't hear past the buzzing of the blood in my ears. I forced myself to take a deep breath, another.

I've had that dream before. When I was very little. I've hidden in the drapes too—please, Mr. Giant, don't—

Thump. Thumpthump. Ka-boom. Crash. The giant overhead, looking for me. But I was awake now! Frozen to the bed, though I was sticky with sweat. I threw the covers over my head so I couldn't see, threw them back. I strained my eyes to see—not that I wanted to see anything.

Clunk. Thump. Directly overhead. Silence. Then thump thump, thump thump, his stick tapping as he slowly looked for me. A light glowed inside somewhere, pale, bobbing—thump thump. I wanted to close my eyes, but they were riveted open. Ka-boom right overhead. I shrieked. The light coming closer. The door opened.

"Jessica. Are you all right?" Agatha's voice. I couldn't say anything, I was so scared. "Jessica?"

I tried to swallow, cleared my throat. "Do you hear—those noises?" The quavering voice didn't sound like mine. If she hadn't heard them—

· "Pesky things. I was hoping we'd be free of them this summer, but they're back."

"What?" I had the bedclothes up to my ears.

"Flying squirrels. They're the noisiest pests, and nocturnal, unfortunately. We must just ignore them. Well, if you're all right, I'll go back to bed."

"Yes, thank you, Agatha. Sorry to wake you."

"You didn't. They did. Pesky things." Her light departed in a wash of exasperated mumbles.

I straightened the covers and rolled onto my side, turned over the pillow and punched it into shape. No giants. Flying squirrels, whatever they are.

What I do when I've had a bad dream or can't go to sleep is recite Winnie-the-Pooh rhymes. *"Have you been a good girl, Jane? Why should I want to be bad at the zoo?"* and *"Whatever's the matter with Mary Jane it's lovely rice pudding for dinner again"* and *"Bears, just watch me walking in all the squares,"* but my favourite is *"I've had my supper and had my supper and HAD my supper and all"*—

Thump. Ka-boom. Crash. I jerked awake, sweating again. I threw off a blanket and rolled over. Thumping squirrels, not flying squirrels. I wished I had my teddy bear. It's blue and pink, and when it was new its tail squeaked. My father brought it for me; we went to meet him at the train and he gave it to me, I carried it all by myself, all the way up the stairs and over the train tracks even though it was as big as me then. I was three. Mum sewed my teddy bear new eyes when the old ones came off and she made him some

43

overalls like mine. Then I was seven? We had a cane in our house at the back of Mum's closet with the blue pin-stripe suits. The cane slipped on the hardwood when I tried to walk with it, scratched the floor. Mum said, "Put it back." Did my father use a cane? Agatha's stick has a big rubber tip, it doesn't slip—big, tip, slip—

Light. The sun shining farther into the veranda than last week. Birds chirping. A fly buzzed somewhere, and the smell of a hot day. I tugged off my nightie, pulled on underpants, shorts, and found my shirt—white with blue cowboy brands. My uncle and aunt brought it from Arizona when I was nine. Mum says it's getting too tight to wear, and it's true. I have to hunch my shoulders to do up the buttons, but it's my favourite shirt. Like a piece of home. I can think I'm a cowboy rounding up cattle, and now it's soft with wear.

Agatha was sitting at the table eating corn-flakes. Which was too bad because I wanted to make her oatmeal. "Good morning, Jessica," she said, as she has every morning. "Did you sleep well?"

"Yes, thank you." I got a bowl and a spoon, sat down and poured myself cornflakes and milk. I watched the cornflakes going onto my spoon so I didn't have to look at Agatha. She slurps the side of her spoon and her lips get slick with milk.

44

"That was a bit of excitement last night. You mustn't let it disturb you."

I chewed, frowned. How'd she know about my dream? "Oh! The flying squirrels!"

"They like abandoned buildings. Frequently after I've been here a week or so they move next door. No one has been in that cottage for years." Agatha's accompanying slurp had disapproval in it. She dabbed at her mouth with her serviette.

Don't rub your lips, Jess, dab. That's ladylike.

Yes, Mum.

"Do they really fly?" Maybe if I snuck upstairs I could see them at it.

"Technically, no. They leap. But long distances. They have loose flaps of skin between their legs— like bats—and they can soar and glide if they take off from heights." Agatha slurped more corn-flakes. She likes them soggy. I eat them fast so they stay crisp. I poured a second bowlful, reached for the milk bottle.

"I have wondered," Agatha said, "if they put on concrete boots at night. Their take-offs and landings are so noisy."

I looked up and grinned. She was pushing a missed cornflake into her mouth and her lips were busy trying to catch it. But the lines around her eyes tilted up. "They go barefoot in the day and put the boots on at night?" I encouraged.

45

"The boots are lined up in a row, according to size." Was she really joking? She never joked in Toronto.

"The squirrels line up and fly into them?"

"Ready, set, go," Agatha said.

I laughed. "We should send them to silent pilot school!"

"But they won't meet the height requirement." Agatha's bosom heaved once and her lips tried to not curve up.

"One of my uncles was a pilot in the First World War. He's really short. I guess they didn't have height requirements then. He was a friend of my father's. That's how Mum met him." I poured another bowl of cornflakes, decided to try again. "Agatha, what was my father like?"

She'd finished her cereal. I leapt up, got the teapot off the stove and filled her cup. "Thank you," she said and took a sip. "He was nice. A nice boy. Good to his mother." She sipped again, put the cup on the saucer. "He came here once, as I recall. With his mother—"

"Here? He was here?" My spoon clattered to the floor. "When? What did he do? How old was he? Where did he sleep?" I knew I was prattling and tried to calm down, but I couldn't. My father here! In this cottage!

Agatha was frowning. I bent to pick up my

46

spoon. She nodded approval. I couldn't eat any more. I pushed my bowl and spoon away. "I don't remember, it was so long ago. He did what everyone does, I suppose. Swam and lay in the sun—"

"Did he swim to the island?"

"Probably. He was a good swimmer."

"But he wouldn't have lain in the sun. Mum says he burned."

"Well, then, he didn't."

I could tell she was losing interest. I had to be quick. "How old was he?"

Her eyes roved the room, lingered on the pump and dishpan. I held my breath. Tell me, I willed.

"Probably shortly after I met Mary—his sister—shortly after they moved to Toronto—she and Robert and their mother came up for a holiday—he was young, very young—probably would have been—thirteen, fourteen, fifteen, around there—" I let my breath out in a huge sigh. She looked enquiringly over her teacup.

"Where did he sleep?"

"That I don't remember."

"On the veranda?"

"Probably not. It wasn't screened."

"Maybe he didn't mind mosquitoes. He was pretty strong, I bet. All that stuff he went through in the war, trenches and poison gas and saving someone to get a medal—" Agatha was looking at

47

me as though I'd flipped my wig. I clenched my teeth so I wouldn't babble on.

"He was just a boy," she said.

I took my bowl and spoon to the sink. I know when a conversation is over. I know when a grown-up isn't going to say any more. But still—

SEVEN

I chopped kindling for the hour I had to wait to swim after eating—I couldn't sit still to read. I thought about going to my cave, but that wasn't where I wanted to be—because—because—that's my private place—where I went to—to get away from him. To not think about him. When he was sick. Now I needed a place I could think about him. The hands of the clock moved so slowly.

Finally I yanked on my bathing suit, yelled good-bye to Agatha and swam out to the island. I pulled myself up on the rocks. The sun was already hot although the air still smelled of early morning. An island is a perfectly safe place. You can see in every direction. No one can sneak up on you on an island.

Now I allowed myself to relax. The revelation that he had been here bubbled up in me so fast I could taste it, like ginger-ale fizz. He'd swum out here. Not much older than me. Maybe even my very age. He'd looked at the cottage from here, exactly like this. He'd sat on this very rock, lain on it. I gently rubbed my hand over it, brushed dirt and grit away. I rolled on to my stomach and threw my arms out, embracing the rock, wishing I could hold all of it, pick it up and cuddle it. I kissed the rock. Then I had to pick bits of grit off my lips. I felt a little foolish. I sat up and hugged my knees.

Grace Kelly, let me introduce my father, Robert Crawford.

How do you do, Robert. You're a bit young to be a father, aren't you?

I laughed out loud. He was really here, Grace Kelly. He was good to his mother. If we'd been here at the same time, maybe we'd have been friends, like Scott and Pete and me. He was a good swimmer—"Come on, Jess, I'll race you to the shore"—he probably would have won, Grace Kelly, he was older than me, and he won medals for running at his school, we have them, they're solid gold.

50

My, he was quite an athlete, Jessica.

Yes. And just think! He was here! Maybe he scraped himself on this rock and some of his skin's still here.

Highly unlikely, Jess. After all these years.

Well, yes, Grace Kelly, but still—

I dove into the water and swam all around the island, then halfway around again and climbed out on the other side. Grace Kelly was waiting for me. Do you think he could have swum over there, to Bigwin Inn?

All across the lake, Jess? Maybe. Don't you try it, not alone.

Slowly, all my happiness and excitement leaked away and I felt as flat as old ginger ale. Why did Mum marry someone so old he got sick and died? Why didn't she marry him sooner so I could have known him? What was the point of making up stories about someone who was dead? Who'd been here once fifty years ago? Introducing him to Grace Kelly? Thank heaven I was alone and no one would ever have to know. Mad at myself and so tired and heavy, I side-stroked back to the cottage. After I changed and hung up my bathing suit, I lay on my bed and read for the rest of the day. Not thinking.

CHAPTER

EIGHT

Mum arrived about nine on Friday night. I hadn't heard the Studebaker. I was down in my cave, and the first I knew her voice was calling, "Jess?"

I'd been expecting her all evening, but just then—or before then—I'd got so tired of being excited, Grace Kelly and I had started to make a garden in our cave.

I nearly cried I was so happy. It's like I have a place to belong every time I hear Mum shout or even whisper, "Jess?" I ran up and threw my arms around her, buried my head in her armpit breast area, somewhere familiar and close and, yes, it was Mum, you can always tell a mum by her smell. Not that I'd ever say that to anyone, not even Grace Kelly. Maybe it's only me, I think, who knows that mothers always smell the same even if they change their perfume. So I smelled Mum close up and thought, for two days I don't have to look after Agatha, Mum can look after both of us. Then I straightened up because I knew Mum had worked all week and had driven from Toronto and I could look after her. She'd need it. So I said, "How are you, Mum?"

"I'm fine." Her voice had its usual sort of half-laugh.

"How was work?"

"Fine. Not too busy. Lots of clients away on holidays." But she looked tired.

"How was the drive up?"

"Fine." She hugged my shoulder and I put my arm around her waist. We started up the steps to the veranda door. "Though everyone and his cousin were leaving the city at the same time."

"Don't be disturbed tonight by noises, they're only flying squirrels. We don't have them in Vancouver, do we?"

"No. Have you gone to the stables this week?"

"No."

"Why not?"

"Oh—" I shrugged. "Have you had dinner?"

She smiled down at me. "I ate sandwiches in the car."

"Do you want some tea?"

"Now that would be lovely! And tell me, how have you managed?"

She brushed my hair back from my face in a very Mum way and I smelled her again and said, "Fine." Just before she opened the door, I said, "Agatha told me my father was here when he was a boy. Did he ever tell you about it?"

"No. Or not that I remember." She gave my shoulders a squeeze. "That would have been long before we met, long, long before we married."

"Why didn't you marry him sooner?"

"I wanted a career. Women couldn't do both then—have a career and a family." She smiled, gave me a final squeeze and opened the door. "Though I would have liked another child, especially if it turned out like you." She greeted Agatha and entered the cottage. I followed her, holding a warm, fuzzy feeling like a blanket.

We had tea and went to bed. I don't know if the squirrels flew or not.

CHAPTER

NINE

Next day after Agatha swept the floor, we drove into Huntsville to get groceries. Dorset is the closest village, but Huntsville is bigger and has an A & P store, although Agatha says the best bread in Ontario is baked in Dorset.

I love driving into small towns, being at that place where the town starts with a cross street and stop signs, yet you know you're still on the highway that's pretending to be a street for a few blocks. I love standing on the main street of a town and being able to see country—hills, perhaps, or mountains, or even fields and trees. Just try to see country when you're standing on a main street of Toronto! Just try to think about country!

In Vancouver you can see the mountains and ocean, but it's not the same as a small town where you can see its edge—exactly where the country ends and the town begins. I especially love towns where the field dust has blown down the main street, and you park your car at an angle into the curb. Towns like these always have general stores with saddles in the window, and I can imagine that if Mum and I lived in a small town, I'd have a horse that I'd ride down the main street and tie to a hitching post while I did the shopping.

Huntsville is a little too big for me, even though I could see rolling hills and the glint of a lake—Mum had to parallel park in front of the A & P. And when we got out of the car, the dust wasn't field dust but hot town dust. The store was crowded. I stopped off at the magazine rack to see if any of the new movie magazines had a story about Grace Kelly—

Why, Jessica, are you reading about me again? I thought you knew everything about me—why, you probably know more about me than I do!

Oh, I doubt that, Grace Kelly. Besides, maybe you've done something new this month—

I don't seem to have, do I? Can you find anything?

No.

You know my father's name is Jack and my

brother's called Kel and I have two sisters and grew up in Philadelphia—

I don't mind reading the same facts over again— oh, here's a new picture of you, oh, it's lovely, Grace Kelly.

Yes, it is stunning, isn't it? It was taken when I went to a benefit ball for Displaced Persons. I believe a movie star has a responsibility to the world—unlike some of my fellow stars, who are only interested in themselves. Oleg Cassini designed that dress especially for me. He even sewed it himself.

It's wonderful. I wish I could wear strapless gowns like you.

Maybe you will, my dear.

And these elbow-length gloves. I like this picture best, the way you're patting your hair—

Oh, that candid shot. Do you like it best? I'm not sure—these photographers sneak up on you in Hollywood, you have to watch yourself every moment. Why, it wouldn't surprise me to find one in the washroom—

Oh, Grace Kelly, I'd never expect you to say something like that!

"What are you smirking about, Jessica? Smirking is not an attractive expression for young ladies."

I closed up the magazine and looked at Agatha.

She was leaning heavily on her walking stick—it's carved with leaves and has a silver handle; she says it belonged to her father—and she looked mad at something. Me, for "smirking"?

But she continued, "I'm going to wait in the car. One used to give one's order to the shopkeeper at the counter, none of this walking up and down aisles. They used to deliver as well." She stomped off in a cloud of mutters.

I considered the magazine, put it back on the rack. Most of it was about Marlon Brando and James Dean, not worth thirty-five cents for only those two pictures of Grace Kelly—though I could get it for Lynn, she's crazy over Brando—

Aren't you, my dear? Everyone likes Marlon. He's the hottest property in town.

I'm not everyone, Grace Kelly, I think he's a slob. I only like you.

A true fan, so loyal. I certainly appreciate it, Jessica.

I found Mum in the vegetables. "Don't buy carrots," I said, then checked what she'd put in the buggy already. Cheese, margarine, milk— "Isn't there any homogenized?"

"Couldn't find any," Mum said.

Ugh, I hate the creamy top of standard milk, the way it slimes in my mouth. Even though Mum pours it off carefully, there's always some left, like the froth on a wave. I never have the first glass out of a new bottle of milk. Now that they're homogenizing it, it isn't quite so slimy. But maybe they don't have homogenized in Huntsville yet.

I hate margarine too—and butter—especially in lettuce and tomato sandwiches, more slime— except I like colouring margarine, popping the dot in the middle of the package and kneading it with my fingers till the orange streaks turn the white lump all yellow. That's my job, to colour the margarine, and I do it while I'm listening to the radio Sunday evenings, "Our Miss Brooks" and "Boston Blackie" and "My Little Margie" and "Jack Benny." Sunday's my favourite radio night. But we don't have a radio at Lake of Bays.

When Mum and I got out to the car, Agatha was asleep. Although Agatha never just "sleeps." She either "reads" or "cat naps" or "passes the night pretty well." This must have been a cat nap since she didn't have a book. Which reminded me of the magazine—should I have bought it?

Mum drove and Agatha sat beside her. When there's just Mum and me, I sit in the front, but now I had the whole back seat to myself. It's long enough for me to stretch out. With my head on the arm rest and my knees bent, I can sleep or look out the window at tree-tops and telephone poles flipping by. But it's a better seat to sleep on in the winter when I'm wearing more clothes. The rough, ridged fabric scratches where my shorts and sleeveless blouse don't cover.

We bought this car last August when we moved to Toronto; it's our first Studebaker. My best school friend Susan's family had a Studebaker. Blue too, but a fifty-two, not a fifty-four. They went to California in it. She brought me back little candied oranges in a miniature crate. The oranges looked better than they tasted—but I didn't tell her that.

Lynn's family has a green fifty-one Pontiac. We used to have a forty-nine Prefect with brown leather seats and if it was parked in the sun, the seats were too hot to sit on. Before the Prefect, I guess we had a Ford. Mum says my father always had black Fords and he called them Betsy. Betsy One, Betsy Two, Betsy Three—those seats were covered in scratchy ridges and the windows were too high to see out. Or I was too small.

Sitting behind Mum, I could see the side of Agatha's face. Her lips stuck out sort of loosely and the hairs on her chin gleamed in the sunshine coming through the window. Her head nodded as if she were agreeing with everything, but I knew she wasn't. Unless she was, deep inside. Maybe getting old is looking yes when you're feeling no. Or looking no when you want to feel yes.

I moved across the seat so I was behind Agatha. Now I could see the way her hair slept last night. And the side of Mum's face—soft like the skin's falling down to her jaw. Mum has lines around her mouth and eyes that move when she talks and smiles. Her hands were large on the steering wheel. Their veins made bumps like dark frozen rivers, and the ring on her little finger was turned so the stone faced me. A bloodstone. My father gave it to her when they got married; it has his family crest carved in it. We studied phrases in school like getting blood from a stone and I'd asked Mum, "How do you get blood from a stone?" She laughed and said she didn't know and not to bother trying, but I still wonder why it's called a bloodstone. A stone with blood on it, maybe?

I love Mum's hands. Mine don't have veins that stick out. But Mum said, "They might when you're older." Then she said, in a different tone, "Though maybe they won't. You're more like your grandmother." She meant my father's mother. She was small too. All my grandparents died before I was born. So maybe that means they weren't my grandparents—just my parents' parents?

Two grey heads in the front seat. Agatha's old grey and Mum's young grey. Mum's hair was sleep-marked too. But her face is alive when she talks. Sometimes when she isn't talking, her face scares me. It looks as if it's gone places I don't know. The way she looked when my father was sick. When I asked why he was sick.

What are you doing with two old ladies?

Mum's not old, Grace Kelly.

She has grey hair.

She's prematurely grey—don't look at me that way, Grace Kelly.

My mother doesn't have grey hair.

I know, Grace Kelly. You have a real family. Your parents married younger than mine did. When you were twelve, your mother wasn't fifty-two. And your father wasn't fifty-six when you were born. Mum's not that old—why, she's eleven years younger than my father was when he died.

How old were you?

Eight, Grace Kelly. In Grade Three.

That's pretty young.

I didn't feel young. I felt as old as anyone.

Why did your mother marry someone so much older?

62

Love doesn't have anything to do with age, Mum says. And that's true or she wouldn't love me, would she?

Yes, she would. You're her child. It's different with children.

Well, Grace Kelly, we've been to Huntsville and now we're going to Dorset and the sun is lightening the side of Mum's face and her hair is curling under her ear. That's the place I like to put my head, right where the skin goes under her jaw down to her shoulder. She smells nice there—lavender. Does your mother use lavender, Grace Kelly?

No.

Well then.

Outside the car, the world was going by. Mainly trees, but enough grass by the edge of the road to ride a horse. There could have been something magical beyond those trees, a grove of flowers or a small pond. But the trees whipped by too fast. If I could only see between them, I could see how to get through. I wanted to call out, Stop, Mum! There's a space! but by the time I'd seen it she'd driven past. So I looked for the next one. But the same thing happened.

And that was how I sat in the back seat. Riding my horse along the grassy edge and looking for spaces between trees.

CHAPTER

TEN

When we got back to the cottage from Dorset and had put the groceries away, we ate grilled cheese sandwiches on fresh Dorset bread for lunch. Agatha announced triumphantly, "There now, Eleanor, am I not right about this being the best bread in Ontario—and probably British Columbia?" Mum laughed and agreed.

Grace Kelly thinks Dorset would be a perfect setting for an old-fashioned movie, with Robinson's General Store on one side of the river and the bakery on the other. Willows hang down over the bank, dragging their leaves in the water. I could have stayed in Robinson's forever. It's old and huge. The wooden steps are hollowed from feet. It has fishing tackle and hardware and food and clothes and real deerskin moccasins. I asked Mum if I could buy a pair, but she said six dollars was too much and how about ice cream instead? If Grace Kelly made a movie here, she'd have to buy moccasins. She'd buy me some too, for showing her the place. Agatha and I had chocolate cones and Mum a maple walnut, and we ate them watching the river from the bridge to the bakery.

The bakery is a wooden shed with an open window and BREAD hand-written over it. They bake the bread right there, inside. It made me think of Heidi, living in Dorset and stealing Clara's white bread. I've never understood why Heidi thought white bread was so great; we always eat white bread. Still, I could be Heidi and Grace Kelly, Clara. But someone should invent odour-movies so the sweet yeasty baking smell wouldn't be wasted.

After lunch Agatha stumped off for her afternoon read; Mum and I washed the dishes. Then Mum said, "Let's go see the riding stable."

In Robinson's she'd inquired: yes, there is a bus that goes down the highway every weekday afternoon at two and comes back at five. All one had to do was stand on the road and wave. I'd listened from behind the fishing tackle so no one would think she was asking for me.

I could easily have waited to take the bus, but I knew Mum wanted to explore. Mum and I spend a lot of time in cars. Sometimes I think she's happiest when she's driving somewhere. Before I was born, before she got married, Mum drove all over British Columbia and up to the Yukon and down to California. She says you didn't have to have driver's licences in those days; all you had to do was buy a car and jump in. She has old brown pictures of her and some friends in front of square, black cars. They're all wearing riding breeches. I think that's odd, but Mum says that was the fashion in the nineteen-twenties. Wish it was now, and not dresses.

Even though we've only owned the Studebaker a year, we've put nearly twenty thousand miles on it. That's double the national average. Each weekend all year, we drove somewhere out of Toronto to explore. We'd pick a town and drive to it and then around it and then we'd stop and have a hamburger and a chocolate malted milkshake. We've been to Guelph and Galt and Whitby and Brantford and Niagara Falls. That was disappointing. I'd expected a higher waterfall. But it was exciting to stand underneath it in a rubber slicker and get wet from the spray. I bought post cards to send to my friends in Vancouver. They'd be impressed.

I wonder if I ever mailed them?

We even went to Buffalo once. I like being in the States. They have all the candies that are advertised in the comic books that we don't have—like Hershey bars and Fat Alberts. We went to California after my father died, and I saw Hollywood and Sunset Boulevard. But I was only eight so I was too young to really care. I hadn't even heard of Grace Kelly. I'd love to go back now. Though I forget when I'm in the States to order fries with my hamburger. When I say chips, they bring the kind out of a bag. And they don't know what gumboots are.

Mum said, "Here's the sign. This is where you get off the bus."

My attention popped up, and I leaned forward. A weathered sign saying *something* stables and a dirt road leading through the trees. Mum turned in. "It might be easy to miss," I said.

"Tell the driver where you want to get off." Mum thought she was being reassuring, but she doesn't know I hate telling drivers where to let me off. It makes me feel dumb.

The road wound up a hill and came out on top in a large clearing. An old stone-bottomed barn with rickety sides and roof beside a gigantic manure pile. Five horses grazing in the pasture. Below sparkled another bay of the lake.

"Do you want to ride?" Mum asked. In the silence of the stopped car, her voice was loud.

"Now? Today?" Suddenly my stomach tickled and the buzzing was loud in my ears. "I thought we were just seeing where the stable is."

"Sure, but you can ride if you want." She smiled as if she were giving me a present.

I found a fingernail that hadn't been bitten for a while and looked out the window. Two of the horses in the pasture were staring at me. I've ridden lots of horses since I took lessons three years ago, but always, between getting out of the car and getting on the horse, I think I don't remember how to ride. Horses are awfully big. They can step on you and bite you and throw you off. And I have to go into the stable and talk to a strange man or strange kids who know what they're doing and the man might not think I can ride and will put me on an old slow horse who won't move no matter how hard I kick, and the strange kids will laugh. I wished we could just drive on to another village. It's safe in the car.

"It's pretty hot for riding," I observed. "Besides, I can't. I'm wearing shorts. I'll get saddle- sores."

"Oh. We should have thought of that." Mum sounded disappointed. In a minute she brightened. "Well, you might as well go look at the horses, make sure they do rent them."

"I can do that another day."

"There's no point in taking the bus if they don't rent horses."

I sighed. When Mum is being reasonable, I don't have a chance.

"Do you want me to come with you?" she asked.

"No!" Strangers would laugh even more if they thought I needed my Mum. "You wait here." My tongue smacked the roof of my mouth. I sighed again, very loudly.

"Don't you want to ride?" Mum asked, puzzled.

How could I explain? Of course I didn't want to—but I did want to. Just—not right now. "Of course I want to," I sulked.

Slowly I opened the car door and got out, closed it slowly behind me, wishing slow would be silent too. Clumps of large white flowers and small blue ones scattered throughout the unmown grass. Hot in the full glare of the sun. We should have stayed at the cottage, gone swimming. Without looking back at Mum, I crossed to the barn's open door. The smell of manure and horse sweat prickled my nostrils.

Inside the barn, I stood, blinking, while my eyes adjusted to the darkness. I hoped no one I couldn't see was looking at me. Flies buzzed loudly. Nearby a horse stamped its hoof. Gradually I could make out shapes between me and the rectangle of sunlight that was the door at the other end. Stalls, a few with horses. No people. My inside buzzing was as loud as the flies. Maybe no one was here. Maybe I'd have to yell—ugh. If no one answered, I could leave. Tell Mum there wasn't anyone. But Mum might want to see for herself and then there might be someone and I'd feel really stupid. And—I do love horses. I walked slowly down the aisle between the stalls. A blockage of light at the other end. A hunched-over shape, thumping, clattering towards me. The giant—my mouth opened to scream. My hand flew up to stop it. I couldn't move my legs and my stomach tickled and churned.

Can't be a giant, you're awake, I told myself firmly. You're in a stable. At Lake of Bays.

The man clanked down his wheelbarrow and straightened. He was huge—tall and broad.

Part of me wanted to run away, part of me wanted to crumple into a heap, another part wanted to fade with dignity back to the car. None of me wanted to go riding very much.

He said, "Thought I heard a car, but I was out back. What do you want? T'go ridin'?"

"Not today." My mouth was so dry I mumbled. I cleared my throat. "Maybe during the week. Do you rent horses?"

The man took a huge hankie out of his jeans'

pocket, wiped his face and his bald head. "What d'ja say? Can't hear you."

"Do you rent horses?" I repeated, feeling stupid, mad. Was he deaf?

"Sure do. Dollar-fifty an hour. Ya ridden before?"

"Yes."

"But not here?"

"No."

"Okay, have t' send Harv with ya, don't want ya lost. Harv! Harv!"

He mustn't have heard me. I felt really stupid. "I can't ride today."

His eyes flicked again, gave me a weird look. "Oh yeah? Why not?"

"Um—my mother's waiting. We have things to do. I'll have to come some other day."

"Ya want me to reserve a horse for ya? I get booked up in the summer with the Lodge people."

Another shape slouched in through the square of sunlight. "Yeah, Bud? Ya called me?" Harv was thin, not very tall, a teenager. I hate teenagers.

Bud ignored him. He was waiting for my answer. Harv looked me up and down. "Okay," I said, keeping my eyes on the ground, backing towards the door I'd entered.

"What day?"

My eyes lurched up to Bud's. "What day?" I echoed.

"What day do you want to ride?" Bud's tone was phony-patient. Harv laughed, a nasty snort. They must have thought I was really dumb.

"Thursday," I snapped, and glared at Harv. He had pimples and a greasy duck-cut. "At three o'clock."

"Okay." Bud pulled a pad and stub of pencil out of his pocket. "See ya then."

I turned and walked down the long aisle, knowing they were staring after me, Harv with a sneer. Thursday was ages away. Anything could happen. The world could end. Agatha could die. The bus could break down. At the least, I just wouldn't have to turn up.

But if you want to ride, you know they'll expect you.

Yes, Grace Kelly.

And it is fifty cents cheaper than Toronto.

Yes, Grace Kelly.

And you know how much you like horses. This is beautiful riding country—see that trail leading into the woods? This spring in Toronto you've biked miles to the stables.

But I know the people at that stable.

You didn't once.

Oh, Grace Kelly! Stop being reasonable! That Harv's a creep.

Mum folded the page corner down, put her mystery into her purse and smiled at me expectantly.

I slid into my seat. "I'm maybe riding on Thursday—it costs a dollar-fifty." Before she could comment, I added firmly, "Now let's go home and swim."

CHAPTER

ELEVEN

After dinner Mum said, "How about a rubber of three-handed bridge?"

Agatha snapped out of her book and grinned so widely she had to adjust her teeth. "What a good idea!"

I wanted to pretend I hadn't heard, but they'd seen me glance up. Keeping a finger in my book, I said hopefully, "Canasta?"

Mum and Agatha were looking at me, eyebrows up in anticipation. There is nothing in this cottage to read but mysteries. No horse books. I was on my sixth Erle Stanley Gardner. Perry Mason was about to go to court and Della Street said Paul Drake had new information. Of course, after six books I've got the plot. Someone kills someone and someone gets arrested and goes to court. Perry Mason gets him off. Paul does the leg work and Della gets explained to.

Mum said, "One rubber of three-handed and then maybe canasta?"

I sighed, put my book upside down on the chair. These books are so old the spines are brittle. The pages are orange. They all cost ten cents. The covers look like old movie posters—Della Street has bright red lipstick and a perfect pageboy. Even her bangs curl under. Her shoulders stick up like padded wings. The men—whether it's Perry Mason or the killer, I'm not sure—all wear hats with wide brims like my father used to.

Mum is passionate about bridge, but I didn't know Agatha was too. The first thing Mum did when we moved to Toronto was find three women to play with. Bridge involves little sandwiches and tea. Mum taught me to play so I could take her hand while she's in the kitchen making tea. Bridge also involves long silences then bursts of wild laughter between hands. When I've gone to bed after the sandwiches, I hate the wild laughter.

I got the cards and spread them to draw for deal, while Mum helped Agatha to the table. Agatha's arthritis gets stiff in the evening. Stiff in the morning too. About lunch time she moves normally.

Agatha pulled the queen, which was highest, so Mum shuffled for her to deal. Actually, I quite like bridge—though not as much as canasta. When I was ten, my best school friend, Susan, and I played canasta every day at lunch. Scott and Pete and I played on rainy weekends. Probably Mum and Agatha will want to teach Lynn bridge next weekend.

What I don't like is chess. Scott and Pete's father taught the three of us, but there's no surprise. You line the pieces up the same way every time and then move in order. Bridge is exciting because each hand is like a present—I don't know what I'll get until I pick it up.

Mum and Agatha were waiting, their cards sorted and held in front of them like fans. "Pass," said Agatha.

"Pass." Mum had on her serious expression.

"Three hearts." Probably I sounded smug. I had a perfect pre-empt.

"Double," Agatha accused.

"Three spades?" questioned Mum. I knew she wanted to be my partner. But I had no spades and was counting that void in my points.

I checked my hand again: seven hearts, an outside ace and nine points, just as Mum had

76

taught me. Should I bid four hearts, taking the chance I'd go down if Mum ran her spades or let Mum have the bid? It all depended on the dummy. That's what I hate about three-handed; you don't get any help from your partner.

"Four hearts," I said.

They both passed and Agatha led—the two of spades, of course.

I turned over the dummy, arranged it. Three hearts, to make ten between us—wow—the ace of spades—got you stopped, Mum—a slough of clubs and the king, queen, ten of diamonds—I rocked my cards close to my chest and grinned. Then I concentrated as I played my cards, taking trick after trick.

"Well played," Mum said, "but you should have bid it. A small slam."

"She couldn't know, Eleanor. With three-handed. And I doubled." Agatha smiled at me and shook her head ruefully. "Well played, Jessica."

"Thanks. We are keeping score, aren't we?" I got up with a little jump of pleasure to find a pencil and paper.

It was Mum's deal. I shuffled and Agatha cut. While Mum was dealing, I thought out loud, "You taught me to play bridge when I was in Grade Three. The year my father died."

"You were in Grade Two when he died."

I watched her deal, card, card, card, card. "I was in Grade Three. Miss Munro was my teacher."

"When I taught you to play bridge, or when your father died?" She picked up her cards.

One of Agatha's fumbled to the floor. I retrieved it for her, without looking at it. "When he died."

"You were in Grade Two. Miss Forester was your teacher. I spoke to her."

"I was eight. In Grade Three." My hands were shoving the table. Hard.

Mum put on her pleasant, I'm-an-adult-and-I'm-going-to-correct-you voice. "Dear, when your father died, you were in Grade Two. I went over to speak to your teacher. Miss Forester."

"Grade Three. Miss Munro." I wasn't going to cry. I glared at her. Hard.

She glanced to Agatha, back to me, picked up her cards. "Dear, when something awful has happened, it's not unusual to forget what year it was."

"I remember perfectly," I snapped. "Grade Three." I picked up my cards. "Whose bid?" I asked, as if I'd forgotten.

Mum sighed, shot me a tight, concerned smile. But I was sorting my cards. She did too. "One diamond."

"Pass," I said. Not a card above an eight.

"Two no trump," boomed Agatha.

78

Mum laughed. "How patient of you to sit quietly with such good cards!"

Or what a busybody. Enjoying our fight.

Agatha bid six no trump. This time she got the dead hand on the table. Mum and I were partners but we had nothing between us.

We played a few more hands. Mum's score went up, mine went down, but I didn't care. I just dealt and bid, shuffled and played. I knew I was sulking, but I didn't care. Finally Mum said, "We don't seem close to a rubber. Maybe it's bedtime?" I knew she was hoping for a smile from me, but I didn't have one anywhere.

I shrugged, threw down my cards, went to the outhouse, brushed my teeth and climbed into bed. When Mum came to kiss me, I pretended to be asleep.

So much for canasta.

CHAPTER

TWELVE

I stayed in bed, reading, all morning. I only got up to go to the bathroom and collect the seventh Erle Stanley Gardner. Mum called me for breakfast but I wasn't hungry. She paused in the doorway and gave me soft, warm looks. I hate those looks. They have questions marks in them that reach out and hook me. I rolled over towards the lake so I wouldn't see them. Later I heard her chopping the kindling. So let her, I didn't care. Agatha came into the veranda with the broom, but she only swept around herself standing in the doorway. I heard her and Mum mumbling, probably talking about me. I didn't care.

Eventually Mum sat down on the foot of my bed. I moved my legs towards the wall so they wouldn't touch her. "How about getting up now? We're driving around to Port Cunnington for lunch." Her voice had a tense smile in it.

"No. I don't want to."

"Oh, come on. It'll be good for you to get away from here."

"I got away yesterday."

"Look, Jess—" She stretched her hand towards my thigh. I rolled away.

"You go. I'll stay here." I was muttering into the book. I could see the words lying on the page, but couldn't see into the pictures they made. Like pretending to read before I could.

Mum was sitting silently, twisting her wedding rings. If she says anything Social Workery, I will scream—

I sat up and made an effort to smile. "You two go. I'd really like to stay here. I'll be fine."

She looked at me, question hooks. I hardened my smile. She sighed resignedly. "You'll make yourself something to eat?" I nodded. "And don't go swimming until we come back." She stood up. A long pause. "Jess?"

"What?"

"Don't go swimming alone."

"I'll be fine. I'm twelve and a half. I can look

after myself. Go and have a good time." Just get out of here. Leave me alone!

Mum leaned down and kissed my forehead, crossed the veranda to the living room. Agatha was hovering in her bedroom doorway. I heard her say, "I wouldn't let her get away with sulking, Eleanor. In my day—"

Mum made soothing noises, but I couldn't hear the words. She took the old busybody's arm and steered her to the back door. If it weren't for her, around all the time, listening—

CHAPTER

THIRTEEN

I waited to hear the car start, move slowly up the dirt track to the road, then—silence. I threw back the covers, leapt out of bed and pulled on my bathing suit.

I stomped down to the lake and stomped into the water until it was chest high, then I threw myself into a crawl and swam to the island. Turned around and swam back to shore. Again to the island, again to shore. Each time my arm hit the water I wished it were hitting Agatha, hitting Mum, my right arm for Agatha, my left arm for Mum, over and over, old busybodies, both of them, what do they know, they don't know what happened, they can't tell me what to think, I'll show them—

You certainly are angry, Jessica!

Oh, Grace Kelly! Get out of my way or I'll hit you, too!

I swam back and forth six times before I finally pulled myself up on the rocks of the island and lay there, panting. The cottage dominated the shoreline. If Mum came back now, I'd really be in trouble. Oh, so what?

As my breathing calmed, I stopped feeling angry. I felt something else—I don't know what— as if nothing mattered, as if nothing had ever mattered. Not sad exactly, though my throat and eyes were tickling with tears, but heavy, weighted down. If I didn't know what grade I was in when my father died, then I didn't know anything.

I lay spread-eagled on my back. I couldn't move, could barely twitch my fingers, there was so much weight on me, weight from the hot sun, weight from the swimming of my arms and legs, weight from—where? A rock dug into my shoulder-blade, but I didn't care. Only a little pain, what was the point of moving? Wherever I moved, there'd be another rock.

Now, Jessica, I'm sure we can figure out logically what grade you were in.

No, we can't, Grace Kelly.

Of course we can. You just have to want to.

Well—I don't think so, but—if you do—?

I do indeed, my dear. First you'd better sit up, or at least roll onto your side. There, is that better?

Yes, thank you, Grace Kelly.

Now if you were eight when your father died, you can figure out what grade you were in, can't you?

I guess so. I was five in kindergarten, six in Grade One— I held up my fingers to count — seven in Grade Two and eight in Grade Three! See? I'm right! Mum's wrong!

But Jessica, your birthday is in January. Your father died in May. How old were you in May of each year?

I counted my fingers again. Six in kindergarten, seven in Grade One, eight in Grade Two—I leapt to my feet, kicked at a tree. Oh, get out of here, Grace Kelly!

Why are you mad at me? I haven't done anything. Are you mad because your Mum was right?

My toe was tracing circles in my wet bathing-suit shape on the rock. No. Maybe a bit, but not much. Mum's right lots. It makes me proud of her.

Then what is it?

I don't know, Grace Kelly. I just feel so—heavy.

85

Blank—heavy. If I've forgotten that, what else have I forgotten? If what I thought was right isn't, what is? My eyes filmed over. Everything went blurry. I wiped at them, sniffed. Nobody cares about me.

I do. Your Mum does.

Oh—I know—but she's never here.

She's here as much as she can be. It's okay to cry. Take my hankie.

I don't want to cry. I clenched my fists, glared over the water to the cottage.

So you'll be angry instead? I never get angry. Your mum says you inherited your father's temper, but he learned to control his.

Don't bug me, Grace Kelly!

I didn't mean to. Why don't you sit down and tell me what you know about your father? That way maybe you'll find out if you've forgotten anything.

I sat. My hand found a stick. I watched it poke at dirt and pine needles in a crack of the rock. The sun felt very hot on my drying shoulders. You sit down, too. Over there, where your dress will stay clean. Are you comfortable?

Yes, thank you, Jessica.

He had heart failure. At night. I was sleeping in Mum's bed with her—I *was* only eight—Grace Kelly nods sympathetically. Mum told me in the morning. She said, "Your father died last night." I said, "I don't believe you" and I ran into his room and there wasn't anyone there. I said, "Where is he?" and she said, "They took his body in the night so we can have a funeral." I said, "You're lying. He isn't dead." She said he was. I was wearing my pink elephant pyjamas. I never wore them again.

The stick had gouged out moss now, and a beetle. It scuttled into another crack.

I didn't know your mother lied. Grace Kelly's tone is puzzled, sympathetic.

Oh, she doesn't! That was awful of me to say that! I apologized. She said it was because I didn't want to believe he'd died. She was still sitting on the bed. I was standing in front of her. I could look into her eyes. Except—they weren't looking at me. They were looking at something awful.

But when you were going to the funeral in the big black limousine, your Mum handed you a hankie and when you asked what for? she said in case you cry. And you said—

I know what I said! I said, "I'm not going to cry." And I didn't.

No, you didn't. You threw the hankie in her lap. You didn't even feel like crying, did you?

No. I whispered to Grace Kelly. That's pretty awful to not even want to cry when your father dies. To—maybe—even—be a bit—glad? I drew in a big breath, which caught in my throat, and I choked. Oh, I couldn't have been that! Forget I said that! Grace Kelly leans closer, puts her arm around my shoulder. I'm not sure if I want it there or not.

What was it like before your father died?

He was sick for a long time.

What was he sick with?

Um—my mind's a foggy blur with boulders sticking up. The answer might be behind one of the boulders, but I could trip in the fog. My face is heating up with shame, I've done something wrong—my whole mind's buzzing—I don't know, Grace Kelly. I realize I'm whispering and make myself look out of my mind and at the lake. Mum says he was gassed in the First World War—he rescued someone and got a medal—Mum says the gas took ten years off his life.

So he shouldn't have died until he was seventy-three?

I guess so. By Agatha's age, he'd still have been dead for two years. That makes her really old.

How long was he sick for?

Oh, years. From kindergarten. Mum says from when we waited for him in Spenser's Department Store—on the hard brown bench by the front door. Waiting and waiting, my gumboots keep slipping off, my feet don't reach the floor, hot in my leggings and coat, but Mum's worried something's happened to him—they closed the store and Mum phoned my uncle to pick us up and when we got home, my father was sitting in his chair wondering where we were.

Why didn't he meet you?

He forgot, Mum says. Then sometimes he was home in bed and sometimes in the hospital. We'd go to visit him—

Long, pale-green halls, doors, scary shuffling men in blue dressing gowns, metal bars like a jail around the bed, white bedspread, long, thin, brown-splotched hand upon it—rows of trees with red leaves and I walk from the door to the street touching each tree in turn, back again on the other side, waiting for Mum—another time he sits outside, funny to wear your dressing gown outside, has a gold cord with a tassel on the end for a belt. Want to pull on it hard so he does something, anything, pays attention to me—Mum holds my hand—

Shaughnessy Hospital, where the War Veterans went—

But at the end he was home, Grace Kelly. He died at home.

And your Mum went back to work when he got sick?

Yes.

When?

I was five.

Who looked after you?

Maids.

Did you like them?

Oh, sure. I guess. Well—no. One spanked me. Another locked me out of the house. Mum fired her.

That must have been awful.

Oh—it wasn't so bad, Grace Kelly. I played outside a lot. I always had my private place under the rhododendrons—for when he starts yelling and throwing things—You had maids, too, didn't you?

Yes, but my mother didn't have to go to work. And my father wasn't sick.

Oh, well. It wasn't that bad. It's over now. Yelling—he did yell. And screamed. And he hit us—no, he didn't. And it doesn't matter, does it, whether I was in Grade Two or Three when he died? I *was* eight.

Grace Kelly's beautiful blue eyes look at me steadily. Her pink lips curl into a slight smile of understanding. Her arm, still around my shoulder, squeezes. Actually, Jessica, I think it does matter. I think you should talk to your mother.

I shrug. I'd better swim back and eat a sandwich now, Grace Kelly. Thank you for your help.

When I stand up, she does too. We look at each other for a minute, then I throw my arms around her waist and lay my head on her upper chest. She hugs me back. It'll be all right, Jess, she whispers, and strokes my hair.

I hope so, Grace Kelly. Though I don't know what *it* she means. I want to stay there forever, but I'm just about to cry and I'd hate to get her dress wet. I dive into the lake. Halfway to shore, I tread water and wave. Grace Kelly waves back.

FOURTEEN

I cut thick slabs of the Dorset bread, slathered them with peanut butter and laid slices of lettuce and cucumber between. While I ate, I thought about hanging my bathing suit on a branch far away, but then my hair would still be wet. I thought about saying I'd washed it, but there was no shower or tub. We did all our washing in the lake. I thought about putting on a dress and pinning up my hair; but I never wore dresses if I could help it, and my hair would still look wet. There didn't seem to be much I could do, so I had another sandwich. And two glasses of milk with the new chocolate powder—Quik—Mum had brought up from Toronto.

I pumped some water, cleaned the kitchen, changed into shorts and a blouse, combed my hair and hung my bathing suit in its regular spot on the line stretched between two trees at the side of the cottage. I made my bed. I put lye down the outhouse hole. There was a lot of chopped kindling, neatly stacked. I went into the house. Awfully silent. Perry Mason lay upside down on the chair, but this plot was so much like the last one, and the one before, that I got the cards out of the drawer and thought about solitaire, but then I started dealing out bridge hands. Cards are very comforting. I turned each hand over in order, sorted and counted, decided on a bid. Then I put the two hands with most points to play with each other and let the losers lose. This way I made three straight grand slams.

The car. Silence. I put the cards away. Slowly voices coming closer. I crossed to the door, opened it.

"Hi. Did you have a good lunch?"

"Yes, thank you." Mum smiled. I had a gush of love. "Agatha met two old friends—"

"They might come to visit sometime."

I grinned at Agatha, nice old lady, she looked

happy. Sleepy but happy. "If they come, we'll have a tea party," I said. "I can make bridge sandwiches." She patted my arm as she passed, leaning a bit on it. I took a deep breath. "Agatha, I'm sorry I was upset and—sulky. I hope you will forgive me."

She stopped, and her hand on my arm stopped also. She straightened a bit and looked at me. For faded green eyes, the look was piercing, beady. "Thank you, Jessica." A single pat. "We'll say no more." She tottered off to her room.

When Agatha's door closed, I turned to Mum. "I'm sorry to you too, I was sulky. I'm also sorry, I did go swimming. I had to." I clenched my fists to keep any quaver out of my voice. "And you were right. I was in Grade Two."

Mum's look was soft, her question hooks pulled in. "It was a tough time for you—"

I cut her off with a wave of my hand.

"You know it's not wise to swim alone." A statement. I nodded. Mum sighed and looked away, a bit sadly. "But I suppose in some sense you are doing it alone. I doubt Agatha could save you. And I'm not here." I nodded again. She looked at me intently. "Please be careful. I worry."

"Don't," I said. "I'm a good swimmer and I am careful."

Mum tried to smile but it didn't quite reach her eyes. "Think you could struggle into that clammy, wet bathing suit and come swimming with me before I have to drive back to Toronto?"

I nodded. She put her arms around me and rested her chin on the top of my head. I leaned against her. My eyes teared up.

CHAPTER

FIFTEEN

Monday was hot and humid. By ten it felt as if the sky were a great blue weight pressing down. Agatha said there'd be a thunderstorm, but in the meantime, she'd go swimming.

Agatha does not swim every day; her swimming is a production. While she got into her large red and blue bathing suit, which she must have bought before I was born—it's some thick knitted stuff with a little skirt—I carted her striped canvas chair, towel, soap, washcloth, blanket, hat and book to the edge of the lake and arranged them. Then I went back to help her.

"Your straps are twisted, " I said.

"Silly things. My arthritis—"

"Would you like me to fix them?"

"It doesn't matter. Oh, well. If you want."

I unbuttoned, straightened, rebuttoned. She took my arm and, leaning on her walking stick as well, paraded slowly to the lake.

I dove in, swam a bit, then rolled over to float on my back. Even in the lake it was too hot to do much else. Last week when I'd worried about leeches seemed long ago. Even yesterday felt faded like an old photograph. Agatha shuffled into the lake, knee-deep, thigh-deep, splashed water onto her arms and rubbed her shoulders. Agatha is all curves and lumps, but they're not the curves and lumps magazines say we should have. There's a lump at the nape of her neck, lumps for her shoulders, her breasts are long lumps that hang down, small lumps for nipples through her bathing suit—I don't look at them— and a very large stomach lump that rolls under to her thin legs. Even her nose is lumpish, and her chin.

She waded out some more until the water lapped around her middle, then launched into a modified breast-stroke with a great out-mouthing of breath that made me think of a whale. As she paddled past, she grinned. "Ah, that's a relief, Jessica!"

Agatha is a good swimmer, though she doesn't

put her head in the water. She can swim out to the island, but she can't pull herself onto the rocks any more, she says. She mainly dog-paddle breast-strokes back and forth close to the shore.

I floated on my back and thought about nothing much. It's harder to float in a lake than in the ocean. Mum said salt buoys you up. I said, "You mean it girls me up." That was when I was younger, of course. Mum said it's really easy to float in the Dead Sea or the Mediterranean. She must have been told that, because she's never been there. She's been to Japan and Hawaii. I hope we can go to New York now we live in Toronto. Mum says ummm but she's not much interested. When I grow up, I'm going to travel everywhere. I bet Grace Kelly's been everywhere.

"Jessica! Please get me the soap." I splashed to shore, picked it up and threw it to her. She glared. "You could have hit me!"

"Sorry," I said, meaning it. I had thrown it gently, and right in front of her, where it now floated, bobbing just beyond her fingers, each time she reached. I waded out, handed it to her. She still glared. "I said I was sorry."

"I'm an old lady, not an outfielder. Just hand it to me, hand it to me—" she muttered on, soaping her forearms. I thought I heard "thoughtless" and "child." I was about to say sorry again, this time sarcastically, but she ordered, "My wash-cloth, quickly."

I waded to shore, back again, handed it to her. Not even a thank you. I swam towards the island so I wouldn't have to look at her, in case I said anything out of my anger. That's controlling your temper, I thought, then I laughed and swam back.

"The soap floated!" I told Agatha.

"Of course. It's Ivory." She was now doing her neck and chest.

"At Dollarton we used special salt-water soap to wash with in the ocean but it didn't float. So Mum was always complaining about how many bars got lost. But I wondered what the fish did? Were the mother fishes pleased to find this soap? Did they make their babies wash? Of course, I was a lot younger then when I thought that," I finished hastily.

Agatha said solemnly, "Maybe in a lake soap keeps leeches away." Her face twitched. I thought she had soap in her eye, then realized she was winking.

"Do you want me to wash your back?" I offered.

"Please. And my hair."

I lathered both while she stood shoulder high in water. "We're the same size," I said in surprise.

"Except you're growing up and I'm growing down."

"What do you mean?"

"Old people shrink."

"I thought they just got stooped."

"Noses grow. Ear lobes grow. Bones get shorter."

I finished her hair. She held onto my arm while she ducked to rinse. When she let go I lathered my hair. Then I did a handstand to rinse it. Upside down, I could see the underside of the soap bobbing like a boat on our waves. Would Mum get shorter then? Had my father? Though he was really tall. I hope my nose doesn't grow more! Mum says my father's family all had big noses. I surfaced and scratched the water behind the boat of soap to navigate it to shore.

Agatha lumbered out, holding her limp washcloth. I took it from her, wrung it out and handed her her towel. Would she have taken her bathing suit off to wash if I weren't here? When she sat in her chair, I asked, "Would you like me to comb your hair?"

"That would be lovely, Jessica." She sounded really pleased. I was pleased. I ran to the cottage for a comb, then stood behind her and very carefully lifted her hair to lay it over the back of the chair. Out of its bun, it is long. I combed as gently as I could. "You have beautiful hair, Agatha, it's so white it's like angel hair at Christmas."

"That is sticky stuff. Is there soap still in mine?"

"No—I mean it looks like angel hair. Tell me if I pull."

"I will."

"When I was little, I stayed with my aunt when my father was sick. I had braids then, I was in kindergarten, and even though she tried not to, sometimes she pulled."

"You haven't so far."

"Good. Maybe I'll be a hairdresser when I grow up."

"Not a suitable occupation."

"Why not?"

"For a lady." Agatha had her eyes closed, the towel pulled up to her chin.

"Maybe I won't be a lady. My aunt's always trying to get me to be a lady—put your coat on this way, don't cross your legs that way—" I was doing a prissy imitation. I thought Agatha maybe smiled. At least, the skin on her cheeks moved upwards.

"What soft, cherubic creatures
  These gentlewomen are!
One would as soon assault a plush
  Or violate a star."

"What's that?" I asked.

"That is a poem, and the who is Emily Dickinson. I don't know if I recall any more—
Such dimity convictions,
  A horror so refined—
Of freckled human nature—"

"I love that!" I must have shouted—Agatha cringed her ears down. "Sorry. What is it—a horror so—?"

"*Refined—of freckled human nature—of Deity ashamed*—I'll have to look it up. Perhaps my old *Emily Dickinson* is in the upstairs bookcase—"

"I'll look, Agatha!" I felt so excited—that sounded just like my aunt—how could anyone think of words like that—"*a horror so refined of freckled human nature*"—

"I know a poem by her, we studied it in school—
There is no frigate like a book
  To take us lands away,
Nor any coursers like a page
  Of prancing poetry.
This traverse may the poorest take
  Without oppress of toll;
How frugal is the chariot
  That bears a human soul!
Coursers mean horses and traverse is to cross, and it's sure true about books!"

"Indeed," Agatha replied. "Although that is one of her weaker efforts."

"Well, I don't know—" I'd stopped combing, began again.

"Listen to this." Agatha intoned, " *After great pain a formal feeling comes—The nerves sit ceremonious, like tombs; The stiff heart questions—* questions—gracious! My mind must be going! Along with my body!"

"Oh, I don't think so," I said, still shivering from those lines.

"My mind or my body? Certainly my body is, I can't deny that—corns on my feet, arthritis in my knees and hips, I have indigestion, and my eyesight—" She shook her head so I would have pulled her hair if I hadn't been working on the ends. "Hard to believe I was considered pretty once." Her tone suddenly wistful.

Well, yes, it is, I thought, then said, "You have such an interesting face—" Whoops, wrong word. What would Grace Kelly say? "You're an interesting *study*, you have a *strong* face—it's full of *character*."

"Oh, well, I'll have to do with that." She sounded pleased. But in a minute she added, "Handsome is as handsome does."

Why does she have to say things like that? I almost tapped her skull with the comb.

103

CHAPTER

SIXTEEN

While Agatha started dinner, I went to look for the Emily Dickinson book. I hadn't been upstairs often; for one thing it wasn't very interesting and for another Mum's room made me miss her too much. She'd left her nightie on the bed. A small spill of talcum powder dappled the carved chest of drawers. I wasn't going to lean over and smell it, but I did. Lavender. Mum. I sneezed hard. Some must have got in my nose.

All the heat of the day had collected up here. I crossed to the window, threw it open and leaned out. The sky was darkening ominously and the lake rolled with little whitecaps that looked like the ocean in a wind. Thin birch trees whipped back and forth against a background of more stately swaying pines. I leaned into the wind and, for a moment, smelled the nose-prickling tang of the saltchuck. My eyes stung with wind-tears as I breathed in that familiar smell, and I felt intensely homesick, not just for Mum, but for Vancouver, for the shack at Dollarton. For Scott and Pete and Susan. For when I was very little. Even for before my father got sick. Black curtains and he's marching, a parade of kilts and bagpipes. Mum picks me up so I can see him, I yell Daddy, Daddy, but he doesn't look he doesn't hear me, Daddy!

I blinked and straightened up, held onto the window frame. I know, Grace Kelly. You don't have to tell me. We are thousands of miles from any ocean. My nose is playing tricks.

When we first moved to Toronto, I was astounded at Lake Ontario. I thought lakes were little things, not like the ocean, so big you can't see across it. One day we went to the Scarborough bluffs and, standing there, I didn't have to pretend hard to be at the ocean. The bluffs are sandy and grassy and slope down to the water like the cliffs at Point Grey, except no trees, so it's more like California. That day was windy with whitecaps and wheeling gulls just like home, and I could smell the salt of the sea. Mum said it wasn't salt, but the moisture in the air, and that, with the wind and gulls, made me think I could smell chuck. But I ran on the sand and slid down the bluffs, watched the gulls and the waves breaking at the shore and I was pretty sure she was wrong. I could smell the sea.

This time last year, I thought moving to Toronto would be exciting, but now I don't let myself think I miss Vancouver. Mum wanted to move. She said we needed a change.

Emily Dickinson. I turned to the bookcase—only a small one with two shelves. Not many books. Just paperback mysteries toppled onto each other, because Mum had piled a number of them by her bed.

Other than this bedroom, the rest of the second storey is unpartitioned, a combined sleeping loft and storage area. The roof slopes down to shallow windows with small panes at the back and sides, but the trees block the light even when it's sunny. Now it was so dim my hand automatically reached up to flick a light switch before I remembered—no electricity. Cots draped in old sheets stand upright like soldiers against one of the log walls. Boxes and chairs are scattered randomly, and under a window is another chest of drawers. It's the sort of room they write about in books, where children play on rainy days until one of them finds a secret passage or falls into another world like Narnia.

Two large bookcases guard the back window. I shuffled over to them through the scattered stuff. Dust had made the floor slippery. I thought, It's been a long time since Agatha swept up here. These books were old, covered in dull browns, maroons, blues and dark greens, with faded titles difficult to read in the dimness. I pulled one off the shelf, tilted it towards the window: a picture of a pretty, ringleted little girl in an old-fashioned dress on the cover. Behind her stood a handsome older boy. *Amarylis*. I opened it. Oh John, I will love you forever. We will never, no never, be parted, my darling. Soppy, but I was awfully tired of Perry Mason explaining things to Della.

By grazing my nose along the shelves and peering, I finally found *Poems of Emily Dickinson*. A tremendous boom. I shrieked and jumped. The book fell onto my toe. I shrieked again, this time with pain. I rubbed my foot against my other calf, then bent down to pick up the book. Sudden brilliant light. My heart beat in my throat. Shadows moving in the corners—ghosts, strangers. I grabbed the books and ran to the stairs, stumbling over boxes, into chairs. Another horrendous boom, another flash. I was down the stairs two at a time.

Agatha turned around from the stove, fork in hand. "Whatever has got into you?"

"Oh, nothing." I rubbed my toe again and tried to get my eyes down to their usual size.

"Rain in a minute." She looked to the window with satisfaction. In her prediction? In the storm?

The one thing I hate about Ontario is thunderstorms. Maybe even more than I hate leeches. And nobody told me about them. Whenever there is one, Mum unplugs the radio and the lights—everything electric. She says forked lightning can come down the cords. At home we have sheet lightning. It just lights up the mountains and trees and houses like a backdrop, but here the lightning zooms out of the sky in jagged gashes as if it's searching for me. Or Mum.

A particularly loud boom. I put my hands over my ears. Agatha said something and turned back to whatever she was stirring.

"What?" I shouted.

"Pardon," she corrected. "I said, move your bed inside for tonight, Jessica. The veranda will be too wet. And close the door after you." She looked out at the lightning blaze. A bit of a smile on her face?

I put the books on the table, pulled the blankets off my bed and struggled it inside. Dark as night and only six o'clock. Still hot and humid, but the wind had cold teeth. I remembered the window I'd opened in Mum's room and dashed upstairs. It was banging back and forth. As I pulled it to, the rain started. I suddenly understood the expression in books: the skies opened. They must have. Buckets poured down. Drops splashed back up about three feet from the veranda roof. My hand, still holding the partly open window, was soaked in an instant. I stuck my head out and breathed in the smell of hot earth and leaves wetly cooling. Thunder boomed. I quickly latched the window and got away from it before the lightning flashed. Maybe this was another hurricane, like Hazel, this year. And people here say it rains in Vancouver!

Dinner turned out to be a glurpy mess of hamburger—Agatha calls it mince—with tinned peas in it—I hate tinned peas—and mashed potato. I ate my way through it by counting the seconds between the thunder and lightning.

Over the drumming of the rain, I shouted, "Do you think this is a hurricane?"

"No."

I shouted again, "Trees get hit by lightning. So do houses. Lightning starts fires."

"Mmm." She chewed another mouthful. Sometimes her teeth click when she chews.

"What would we do if lightning started a fire?"

She shifted her mouthful, swallowed. "Depends on how close it is."

"Here. Right here. This cottage. Or a tree just outside." I couldn't eat any more.

"We would calmly go down to the lake and immerse ourselves. We would wait until help came or until the fire had burned itself out."

I picked up my fork, separated some peas from the hamburger and potato. "Has lightning ever hit anything here?"

"No." She chewed and clicked a bit. Then she put her fork and knife down and looked directly at me. "How could I forget! My mind must be going. Of course something was hit! Years ago, a tree right over there." She jerked her head in the direction of the cottage next to us. "It did start a fire!"

I felt breathless with her excitement. "What did you do?"

"We formed a bucket brigade up from the lake. This was before the last war and I had a group of friends visiting, fortunately. The rain started soon but we kept on, worked for hours, and between our water and God's"— Agatha smiled tightly— "we put it out before it spread too far. I think you can still see the damage. I could a few years ago. But if that hadn't worked, we were prepared to go down to the lake and immerse ourselves. It was a

110

frightening experience." She picked up her fork, loaded it, commenced eating. Her eyes sparkled like rhinestones and I didn't know if she were eating this meal or one back then.

Didn't matter. I could see it—a line of men and women heaving buckets from one to the other, sweat streaming from their fire-blackened foreheads, the sizzle of water as it hit the blazing, crackling trees, Agatha in her Grace Kelly *High Noon* dress first in line, the one who poured the water on the fire, who suffered the most steam leaping up on her—

Stand back, all of you! This is my cottage, my only home! My father built it and I must protect it for his memory! I will be closest to the fire!

No, no! You can't! I will!

That is a gallant offer, Robert Crawford, but it is I who must take the risk—

My father wasn't here.

But he could have been.

Agatha, you must stay back! I will be closest to the fire, just as I was in the war!

No, Robert, it is my place to save my home!

Agatha, I will brook no argument. After all, it was I who won a Military Medal in the Canadian Expeditionary Force defending freedom and justice and cottages like this—

Oh yes, Robert. I had a momentary lapse.

Agatha wipes her exhausted, blackened brow. The fire crackles ever closer. You know I take orders from no one, but I respect your experience in these matters. You may take charge—

Agatha had her tongue under her bottom teeth, fishing out a piece of something. They clacked against her uppers and her chin stuck out even more. Rain drummed loudly down. I cleared the table and fetched dessert—tinned mandarin slices and wonderful Dorset cookies with peanuts in them. By now I was having to count higher between thunder and lightning, so the storm was retreating across the lake.

I washed up, as Agatha calls doing the dishes. Eventually we moved to the comfortable chairs. I picked up the *Emily Dickinson*—but didn't open it.

"Agatha!" I heard the intense command in my voice and tried to pull away from it, but it kept on going. "What was my father like when you knew him?"

CHAPTER

SEVENTEEN

"I see you found my book," Agatha observed.

"Oh—yes." I was waiting.

Agatha rocked gently, her eyes half-masted. The rain drummed a gentler roll.

"Agatha," I implored.

"I'm thinking."

Looks like you're sleeping. But I didn't say it.

"What was your father like?"

Good. You remember the question. "Yes?"

She snapped her chair and her eyes up. "You must remember, Jessica, I'm an old lady."

I nodded. Wanted to say, I remember every day, and please don't die this summer.

"—and that I was much older than he."

She was still staring at me, not rocking. My

fingers under the Emily Dickinson cramped. I wiggled them. Please, I thought to Agatha.

"—and that I didn't meet the family until they moved to Toronto."

I nodded. "They were up north somewhere. His father was a minister."

"Rural Dean of Emsdale Parish. Not far from here."

"Really?" I nearly jumped out of my chair.

"Relatively speaking." She was rocking again.

"Did you know him?"

Rock, rock. "Who?" Very faintly.

"My grandfather."

"No. I told you, I didn't meet them until they came to Toronto. That was after he died."

Rain. Rocking. For a second I wasn't sure who she meant had died. I assumed my grandfather. That is—my father's father. "Agatha, *please*," I said again.

"Please what?"

"Oh, Agatha! Stop drooping! This is important!"

She snapped her eyes up, but only once. "Jessica, I deplore your manners. Most unladylike."

"Well, deplore away, Agatha!" I fumbled open the book, found the index, turned to the right page, read, breathlessly, *"What soft, cherubic creatures*

114

These gentlewomen are!
One would as soon assault a plush
Or violate a star."

She recited with me, *"Such dimity convictions,*
A horror so refined
Of freckled human nature,
Of Deity ashamed,—"

I shivered, Agatha had stopped rocking, but by now I didn't care because I'd come to the last verse. *"It's such a common glory,*
A fisherman's degree!
Redemption, brittle lady,
Be so ashamed of thee."

That didn't make much sense to me, but it seemed to make sense to Agatha. She snapped all of her upright and beady-eyed me, perhaps glaring.

I said, hesitantly, "I like 'such dimity convictions'—"

"All right! All right! I will not say 'ladylike' to you again this summer, Jessica!"

"Oh, it's been okay," I mumbled.

"I've overdone it. Some of the lady is good, but most is not useful." She paused, rocked once and her voice changed. "And I suppose you're in a different generation now."

"I suppose," I ventured, surprised, uncomfortable. Agatha apologize?

115

"You will help me to the outhouse," she commanded.

I put the book beside me and sprang out of my chair. Maybe Agatha commands when she doesn't want to ask. Anyway, the steps would be slippery with the rain. I took her arm.

"I don't need help yet," she snapped.

I shrugged and sighed. Loudly.

"In a minute," Agatha mumbled. "In a minute. Bladders. Kidneys. Bodies." She sighed heartily.

"At least you have an excuse," I said.

"What do you mean?" We were nearly at the door.

"Your age. What do you do if you're my age and have to go to the bathroom and you don't know where it is? I hate having to ask!" My voice had risen a bit. I hadn't meant it to.

She threw her head back and cackled a laugh. It ended in a coughing fit. She patted my arm. "I don't know, my dear. I don't know. But thank you for reminding me that bladder worries aren't only the prerogative of old age!"

When we were again seated and Agatha had resumed rocking, she said, "I really didn't know your father well. It was his older sister, Mary, who was my friend. Robert was just a schoolboy, twelve, thirteen, perhaps fifteen. He was polite enough, but mainly palled around with his chums.

As I recall, he was quite an athlete, won medals for his school—"

"Oh, yes!" Goose-bumps on my arms. "We have them still. They're gold—1903. The year Mum was born!"

"Yes. He was handsome too, tall, striking, very well spoken. And well spoken of." Agatha smiled. Her face was softer than I'd seen it. "Mary and I were very close. It was she who introduced me to Emily Dickinson's poetry. We read it together." Agatha's eyes were closed and her voice wistful.

"Did Mary have a big nose?"

Agatha glanced at me. "Gracious, no! What would you ask that for? She had a fine nose. It fitted her perfectly.

"I was upset when her mother—your grandmother—decided they would all move to Vancouver. That would have been 1909 or '10. Everyone was trekking west then." She sniffed with disapproval. "I suppose Robert must have been out of school—?"

I did some fast arithmetic. "He would have been twenty-three in 1910."

Agatha nodded, but without enthusiasm. Obviously my father was not her main interest. "Oh yes, he'd gone into business. Opened a dry-goods store, but it didn't do well. Not that there was any

117

scandal, just—the wrong part of town." She sniffed. "I missed Mary very much. We'd been close friends for ten years. We holidayed in New Brunswick and New York and came here every summer—as going-away gifts, we gave each other copies of Dickinson's poetry." She paused, then added, "That book that you are holding was from her."

I opened the cover. On the flyleaf was inscribed, in faded, spiky writing: To my darling Agatha, with all my love, your friend forever, Mary. And underneath: My reason, life, I had not had, but for yourself.

I felt embarrassed, as if I'd looked into a room I wasn't meant to, but I thought, Friends were sure soppier back then.

Agatha was mumbling.

"What?" I asked. "I mean, pardon?"

"I had been hungry all the years; My noon had come to dine; I, trembling, drew the table near, And touched the curious wine." She was rocking slowly, with a gentle smile below closed eyes.

More Dickinson, I bet. "What happened then? Did you see her again? Or my father?"

"We had certainly planned to, but the war intervened—"

"When you say it like that—the war—I don't know which one you mean."

"The Great War. The War To End Wars."

"It didn't. But you mean my father's war. World War One. That's how we study them in school. One and Two."

"Yes."

"He was a hero. He won medals. I remember a parade and black curtains."

"Do you?" Agatha asked. "Of course, in Vancouver you had black-out curtains in the last war."

"But that wasn't the last war. My teacher said Korea was the last war. It's hard to keep all your wars straight."

"World War Two, then."

"What did you call them—black-out curtains?"

Agatha nodded. Her eyes closed, but she was still rocking.

"I hated them, they were scary. Mum wouldn't turn lights on so she wouldn't have to close them." I was surprised at my gush of memory. "But my father closed them. They were heavy and dark with frayed bottoms I pulled threads out of. Started in one corner and I could pull the thread all the way along—like a train on a track chug chug—" Was Agatha smiling? "My father got mad at me for that, he said Mum should have hemmed them, but Mum said the war won't be won by hemming black-out curtains—"

Where do memories come from? He was wearing a pin-stripe suit, not a kilt!

Agatha was saying, "We said we'd win the Great War by knitting socks. I knitted so many socks. After the war, I never knitted again."

"My father was a hero of that war," I offered.

"Yes." She clicked her teeth. What was in her tone?

"Wasn't he?"

"Yes. I said, yes."

"You knew him. Aren't you pleased he was?"

"Nothing about war pleases me."

"I know it's not good, but he was a hero. We have a picture of him with his medals—"

Agatha sighed. "It's complicated, Jessica. Maybe—"

"No! Don't tell me I'll understand when I'm older!"

Agatha snapped up and glared. She'd been going to, I was right. But I did feel guilty about my bad manners. Slowly, Agatha stopped glaring and nodded. She breathed out heavily. So did I.

She said, "Maybe it's no more complicated than you said. War is not good and some men are heroes. Maybe you'll figure it out. I haven't been able to. But no one ever mentions the sacrifices of women in wars. The deaths of women."

Don't they? I'd never thought about it. They

don't on Remembrance Day at school, just poppies and two minutes of silence—

I got up and put more wood on the fire. Still raining. When I sat down again, I curled my legs up to the side. I searched for a topic Agatha wanted. "Did you see Mary again?"

"Yes, but not until after the war. Travel was not so easy in those days as it is now, no hopping on and off planes, being somewhere in a few hours. And we both had obligations to our families. It wasn't until 1919 that I took the train to Vancouver—a four-day journey. Mary had just nursed her mother—your grandmother—through the influenza epidemic. Her mother survived, but as an invalid, and Mary was very frail and run down. While I was there, Mary came down with the flu. She died within three days. In my arms." Agatha rocked, then added, in a low voice, "I have always been thankful that I was able to be with her, at the end."

My heart thudded and almost-tears tickled my nose. Two tragic deaths: her fiancé's and her friend's. Agatha's young blond head bent over the tragically youthful dying aunt I never knew—

But Agatha would have been forty then. So would have Mary. My father would have been over thirty.

"Mum says he lived with his mother until she died—"

"Yes. She was quite a woman, Mrs. Crawford. Wore nothing but black from the day her husband died—for at least twenty-five years. The family did as she demanded. I wanted Mary to stay in Toronto, but her mother said she needed her—"

"When you visited in Vancouver, was my father there?"

"Robert arrived home just in time to see Mary."

"Did he say anything about the war?"

"Refused to speak of it." Agatha sat up a bit and looked at me seriously, kindly. "This was not uncommon, Jessica. Many of the men refused to speak of their experiences overseas, especially to their families. They wanted to put the war behind them—and to spare the weaker sex." She said the last with a twist of her lips, one of her own jokes.

"Robert wrote to let me know that Mrs. Crawford had died, which was very kind of him—"

"The way you wrote Mum when he died."

"—then, whenever he was in Toronto on business, he rang me up and came for lunch. He was very upset he couldn't go overseas for the second war—"

"Why couldn't he? Because he was too old?"

122

"No. Some men of his age and experience went. It was because he'd been gassed too badly. He was so pleased your mother agreed to marry. They'd known each other for years—"

"He was a friend of my uncles'—they're older than Mum." I was leaning forward in my chair.

"Yes." Agatha was still rocking, smiling with her eyes closed. "When he was in Toronto just after your birth, he said, 'Agatha, I have a daughter! The loveliest daughter! She's beautiful and clever, and we're calling her Jessica Mary.' He described you to the minutest detail."

Agatha looked at me, smiling. Every hair on my arms and legs was standing straight up. I wanted to cry, to laugh, to be alone, to throw myself in her lap.

"A very fine man, your father. A gentleman. And, yes, a war hero. It was so sad he had to die that way, so hard on your mother—"

"What way?"

"Oh—lingeringly. Relatively young."

"I thought he died of heart failure."

Agatha gave me the look: an adult considering a child. "I suppose he did—ultimately. And now, I am going to bed." She heaved herself out of the rocking chair, held onto it until she had her balance, then took a tottery step. She looked tired, old.

"Shall I help you?" My offer was partly automatic.

"I can manage. But I will take that book."

I put the *Emily Dickinson* in her outstretched hand, watched her shuffling manoeuvres from chair to table to wall. I blurted, "Agatha, I'm sorry about Mary."

She stopped, turned. "Thank you, Jessica. So am I, tonight."

CHAPTER

EIGHTEEN

After she closed her door, I continued to sit in the chair, watching the flame flicker in the coal-oil lamp. The rain had softened to a patter. The cottage, its corners dark where light from the fire or lamp didn't reach, felt very large. I felt very small.

A fine man, your father. But—that way of dying? What way? How had he lingered? Hadn't he had heart failure? Maybe Mum and I could drive to Emsdale sometime. Maybe next weekend.

Well, Grace Kelly, what do you think?

I told you. I think you need to talk to your mum.

Do you think this is like thinking I was in Grade Three?

It could be, Jess. There could be things you don't know.

People should tell children things.

I agree. If I have children, I'll tell them everything.

But Grace Kelly, you're not going to have children. You're going to stay a movie star.

Grace Kelly tinkles a laugh and stares regally into space. I can have children and be a movie star.

Sometimes I wish I were your child. (No, I don't, Mum, not really.)

Grace Kelly hugs me. I invited you to visit me in Hollywood.

I know, but I'm looking after Agatha. Do you think she might die?

This summer, you mean? Oh, Jess, I hope not!

I opened the door to go to the outhouse, but it was so dark and such a long way. I bet Grace Kelly never has to go. I squatted by the steps. No one to see me and the rain would wash it away. But someone could be sneaking up behind. I looked around. Trees loomed over me, gigantic and ominous. Branches creaked and moaned. Leaves rustled like footsteps. Raindrops tickled coldly on my bare skin. I tried to pee as fast

126

as possible, but whenever I do that, I slow down.

I blew out the lamp and climbed into bed. The fire seemed to grow in the fireplace. I sat up to check that the screen was in front. Then I lay there listening to the crackle and hiss when raindrops fell down the chimney. My mind was going around in a churn—Agatha, Mary, my father, how had he died? I could see the picture of him as it had hung in the hall in Vancouver, tall in his kilt and plaid, unsmiling, light playing on his blond hair, on the long planes of his cheek-bones, glinting off the cairngorm by his knee. Where was the picture now? Not hanging in our Toronto apartment. Why not? I wished Mum were here, even wished I could crawl into bed with her.

I recited my favourite Winnie-the-Pooh rhyme.
I've had my supper,
And had my supper,
and HAD my supper and all;
I've heard the story of Cinderella,
And how she went to the ball;
I've cleaned my teeth,
And I've said my prayers,
And I've cleaned and said them right;
And they've all of them been
And kissed me lots,

They've all of them said "Good-night."
So here I am in the dark alone,
There's nobody here to see...
Here I am in the dark alone...there's nobody here
but me—

Well, who would there be?

Oh, Grace Kelly, you don't understand!

Aren't you supposed to be alone to go to sleep?

Of course.

Well? Who would be there?

Bees buzzing everywhere. I thought at first it was the fire, but they were much louder than that, louder than the rain, then I thought they'd come out of the rain, out of the fire, but I knew it was the bees and my stomach was tickling into a heave. I was hot, sweating, but too scared to throw the covers off. Somewhere Grace Kelly just kept on asking: Who would be there? Who would be there? Like the wheels of the train that took us to Toronto.

I rolled over and stuck my head under the pillow but my hair caught in my mouth. I rolled back and knew I had to lie as still as possible. Too hot. I wanted to stick my feet out, but I knew that wasn't safe. The bees buzzed on and I was panting. Then tears were running from the outside corners of my eyes, down onto the pillow and I answered her: My father. My father was there.

He came into my room and touched me, my forehead, my arms, my feet, my legs, my stomach, tickling little touches, he pulled the covers off me and I had to pretend to be asleep. I was sobbing now, trying to keep quiet so Agatha wouldn't hear, so my father wouldn't hear, so I'd be left alone, in the dark alone. Then Mum came and she pulled him away. She said, Robert, she's asleep, you come away, and Mum touched my forehead, not tickly like his, but a firm and loving Mum touch and covered me up and still I pretended I was asleep.

I sobbed into my hands, the blankets, wanted to wail and scream, but too scared to make a noise, so scared—I'd had my supper, I should have been alone—

So there, Grace Kelly! And you keep your mouth shut about it! Agatha said he was a fine man!

That didn't really happen—fathers don't do that.

But he did. I know he did. He touched me and tickled me and I hated it. I was scared.

I wanted to sob more, but I couldn't. Why would he have done that? Why didn't Mum get mad? She just led him out.

I wanted Mum so much. I felt so alone, my stomach hurt. I might throw up. I felt so awful I even thought of climbing into bed with Agatha. If I'd had my flashlight, I would have read a book, but I'd left it on the veranda. So I had to lie there, listening to the fire and the rain and the lake waves moaning and churning, crackling and hissing, and all I could think of was his tickly touch and the sound of bees.

CHAPTER

NINETEEN

Thursday morning I sat in my cave and muddled about whether to go riding. I'd been sitting here most of the time since the ground dried on Tuesday, muddling about everything to do with my father, so it was a relief to have a different muddle. First I thought: I'll go riding and then I thought: I'll skip it and then I thought: I'll go riding and then—

You don't have to make a decision, Jessica. You can just sit here until it's too late.

But I want to ride, Grace Kelly. I just don't want to go there. I wish the horse would come to me. We both laugh. Why don't you make any movies with horses in them?

There were horses in *High Noon*.

But you didn't ride them. Just the men did. You mainly wrung your hands and fetched guns.

It was an early picture. Before I won the Oscar for *The Country Girl*.

I didn't mean to offend you, Grace Kelly. Though I must say *The Country Girl* wasn't my favourite movie. You looked so ordinary in that ugly housedress and apron, the way you had your hair pulled back. You could have been anybody. And you weren't happy.

That movie was art, Jessica. The role stretched me!

I reach for her hand and squeeze it. Sorry if I hurt your feelings, Grace Kelly. Guess I like you better unstretched. After a second, she returns the squeeze. I wish two horses would come to us and we could ride together.

That would be wonderful, Jessica! I'd love to go riding with you!

We could ride down the road to the stables and along that trail. If you can't ride, I could teach you.

Would you? I don't ride as well as you. In fact, sometimes I'm scared of horses.

You don't have to be, Grace Kelly. I know they're big, and it feels like you're high off the ground, but if the horse knows you're the boss, it's okay. That doesn't mean hurting the horse, just being firm.

I'm glad you've told me that. I'd like to go riding.

So would I, Grace Kelly. So I guess I'll go.

I'll come with you if you want, Jessica.

Okay. Do you have a riding habit?

No, but Oleg Cassini can design me one this morning—with black gloves instead of white. I'd ask him to make you one too, but there isn't time. You'll just have to wear your jeans.

After lunch, I told Agatha where I was going and walked up to the road to wait for the bus. Since the storm, all the leaves along the trail looked washed and shiny, and in the clearing where Mum parks the Studebaker, more flowers had popped up. But the grass at the edge of the road was already dusted over again from passing cars, and the sun beat hotly down. I lounged against a tree. Up the road was a hill; I'd see the bus come over and could step to the pavement in time. Should I wave my arms to stop it or just stand there? I feel silly waving my arms.

Carefully I pulled up a piece of grass so its juicy stem wouldn't break, and chewed it. An engine noise. I stepped forward. Growing louder.

From the wrong direction. I leaned against the tree again, smelled the car's exhaust clutter up the freshness, listened to silence return. The road had oblong patches of darker tar, coffin-shaped. Suppose someone killed someone and dug up the concrete in the middle of the night, put the body in and patched it over with tar. That would be a bit like *Rear Window*.

It would have to be someone who worked for the highway crew and knew how to mix tar.

Well, Grace Kelly, you could do that.

Ugh. It's too dirty a job.

You could wear work clothes with heavy gloves. Like a uniform. You could make a war movie, Grace Kelly.

No! I never would!

Not even if someone wrote the script just for you?

No! She claps her hand to her breastbone. Never!

I agree with you, Grace Kelly. If my father hadn't been in the war, he wouldn't have been gassed and then maybe he wouldn't have tickled me.

Another engine—from the right direction. A truck crested the hill, sped by. This was boring. I looked at my watch: five after two. Maybe I'd missed the bus. A bird sang somewhere, then a squirrel chittered. Hardly any breeze. Hot. I picked another piece of grass, tasted its greenness. Maybe I should skip it, just go swimming.

Another engine. I walked to the road. This time a van, maroon under its dust. I half-turned away as it barrelled towards me. It slowed, changed gears as it drew nearer. A small sign in its front window, the writing faded. As it passed, I read the sign in the side window: Bus. I was so surprised I just watched it chug on until it was so far I'd have had to run and yell and wave my arms wildly. I kicked the side of the pavement. Whoever heard of a van for a bus!

I felt stupid—and disappointed. Now I wanted to go riding so much I could taste it. I clumped down the trail, changed into my bathing suit and swam out to the island. I swam back and tried to be interested in my book, but the words wouldn't hold still.

When Agatha woke up from her afternoon read, I said, "No one told me the bus wasn't a bus!"

"Oh dear." I was gratified by how sorry she looked. "Perhaps no one did."

Next afternoon, I positioned myself again and waited. When the van barrelled over the hill, I ran to the side of the road and stuck my arm out in a sort of wave. The driver obediently stopped. I asked, "How much?"

"Ten cents." He took my dime and I sat down. There were two long seats behind him and no passengers. The back was full of grocery cartons and taped-shut boxes. I guessed the "bus" was mainly a delivery van.

"Where ya want off?" the driver asked. I told him. A good thing he asked, because there was no cord to pull and, at the speed he was going, I wouldn't have seen the sign for the stables until we were past it. I crossed my fingers so he wouldn't mention yesterday.

When he stopped to let me off, he said, "Ya going back up this aft?" I nodded. "Be over there about five, eh? I'll look out for ya but I won't wait." He almost smiled and I almost liked him.

A hot trudge up the hill. The pasture, barn and manure pile—even larger. A man and two women stood in the stable yard, the women holding saddled and bridled horses. I wanted to turn back and wait until they'd ridden off, but maybe they'd seen me. I'd look stupid if I turned now, so I kept on, slowly.

Harv emerged from the stable with a third horse clumping behind. He handed its reins to the man, who was wearing a bright yellow shirt, new jeans and brown leather shoes. The woman holding the chestnut must have modelled for a make-up company, she had so much on. Her hair was piled up in little gold curls—bleached, I bet—and she wore a sleeveless top, so low-cut I could see cleavage, like Marilyn Monroe's. She too had stiff new jeans, and sandals. The other woman had a brown pony-tail and wore a flowered shirt, older jeans and sneakers. She delicately held the reins of a thin bay.

Harv saw me, gave me a long sneer up and down. "You were s'posed to come yesterday. Where were ya? I had a horse ready."

I shrugged, shoved my hands in my pockets. "Couldn't make it."

"S'pose ya wanna ride now?" I shrugged a nod. His lip curled in an Elvis imitation as he took a rat-tail comb out of his back pocket and ran it through his duck-cut. What a creep. He must have used the whole tube of Brylcreem at once.

"Ya have t'go out with us then, jus' let me get another horse." His reluctant, phony drawl trailed after him into the barn.

Well, don't trouble yourself. I tried to look as sneery as he.

The man was boosting the make-up woman into the saddle. From the way he did it, from the way she was giggling and looking as if she were climbing a ladder, I knew they couldn't ride. I didn't want to go with them. We'd have to walk most of the way and they'd shriek if a horse trotted or wriggled its skin because of a fly. They'd pull on their horses' mouths. The man would want to gallop, in spite of the heat. I thought about leaving before Harv came back, but I'd have to wait on the road for two hours for the bus. I sighed, kicked at a dried horse ball and supposed Grace Kelly would regally make the best of it.

Harv clumped a large, dirty white gelding out of the barn. His hipbones stuck up and his ungroomed forelock fell into his eyes. I patted his nose. He blew out of his nostrils and chewed his bit with resignation. I knew this sort of a horse—a slow plug with a hard mouth. But all horses have something lovable about them.

Harv gave me a leg up into the military saddle. "What's his name?" I asked, though I bet I knew.

"Silver." Right.

The man chortled, "Hi-ho and away." This was going to be worse than I thought.

I shortened my stirrup leathers and gathered up the reins, hoping I looked professional. Harv reappeared, leading a dainty bay mare with a bridle and no saddle. He flung himself onto her bare back and yanked her around in a circle.

Show-off. She half-reared and rolled her eyes. Too bad he didn't fall.

As Harv trotted the mare past me, he said, "You take the end of the line." He told the women and man to follow him. The make-up woman was holding the reins upside down with her elbows out. The other clutched her horse's mane. The man had watched westerns; he lolled back in his saddle so his feet nearly touched the horse's shoulders and gripped the reins in one huge fist. I bet he thought horses galloped straight out of the barn and on forever. Harv should at least have told them some things, for the horses' sakes. But I was pleased he realized I could ride, putting me at the end.

The three fell into line behind Harv. I wondered if Silver had gone to sleep. Finally he ambled forward until his nose touched the tail of the chestnut in front. I had to yank him back. I was right; he had the toughest mouth I'd ever had to haul on.

But at least I was riding. I pushed my heels down and my thighs against the saddle and took a huge breath of delicious sun-warmed horse and leather. I patted Silver's neck and whispered, "Good boy." He threw his head up and jiggled his bit.

If he were my horse, I'd groom him until he

shone, then ride out on this trail alone through the birch-dappled light. Grace Kelly would say, What a good horsewoman you are, Jessica.

Oh, it's not just me, it's Silver. He knows what I want to do before I do. We're partners.

I'd love to ride him sometime.

I'm sorry, Grace Kelly, but Silver doesn't let anyone else ride him. He's temperamental.

I hauled on the reins; Silver again had his nose on the chestnut's flank. I was afraid we'd get kicked, and the stupid woman just swayed on with her elbows out.

We headed downhill along a dirt trail. The lake glinted blue somewhere ahead. Birds sang and saddles creaked. I could see the alternating flanks of the chestnut ahead, and the whole happy world was the joggly motion of me on a horse.

At the bottom of the hill, Harv splashed through a shallow creek and began to trot into a meadow. The other horses trotted, too. The woman on the chestnut gave a shriek and clung to his mane. "Go up and down with his gait," I said, beginning to post. But she went back and forth.

Harv nudged his mare into a canter, and the rest of the horses followed. Silver trotted faster. And faster. Eventually he lumbered into a canter and my teeth stopped rattling. The man, waving his arm over his head, shouted, "Yi-yi-yi!" and his rangy black speeded into full gallop. The other woman was totally wrapped up in her bay's mane. Her feet gripped his ribs as he tried to keep up with the black. I guess she didn't know that would make him go faster. Silver lumbered after the chestnut's rear end. I would have really enjoyed cantering with the wind in my hair, the sound of Silver's breath and squeaking leather, the motion of his body, except I was too worried about the woman on the chestnut. By now she'd lost her stirrups. She slid from side to side as if she were polishing the saddle. The reins flapped loosely; her hands couldn't hold both them and the mane. Harv never once looked back. I guess he was racing the man.

Finally the end of the meadow was safely upon us. I could feel Silver slowing and was ready to post when he bounced into a trot, still with his nose clinging to his friend's tail. The man hauled up his black—as if he needed to—and swung around in his saddle. But his grin dropped as he watched the make-up woman slip slowly down the side of the jogging chestnut, who immediately stopped and began to graze. The other woman managed to stay on, but it took my holding my breath for her to do it.

"Are you all right, Josie?" the man asked the

woman. She gave him the look to kill as she got to her feet.

"No, I'm not all right, you stupid nut! I've never been so scared in my life! What did you do that for—gallop off like the Lone Ranger?" Maybe these two were husband and wife.

The other woman had let go of her horse's mane and gathered up her reins. Too tightly. When her horse put its neck down to graze she catapulted forward. I knew by her "oof" she'd got the pommel of the saddle right in her stomach. Silver, of course, was used to grazing here. I let him.

Harv rode the mare closer to the chestnut, who edged away. I knew that sort of horse, too. We could be here for hours, catching him. Trail rides.

If I come again, I'll go out alone—and I'll ask to ride the little mare. Neat-boned and small and fast. Too good for Harv.

Finally he hopped off her and herded the loose horse closer to Silver, who, for the first time, wasn't interested. I tried to grab the chestnut's reins, but they were hooked down over his ears, grass level. Harv got hold of them and yanked. I was probably the only one who could hear him swearing. He led the horse, its ears flopping, over to the woman, but she yelled, "If you think I'm getting on that animal again, you're crazy!"

"Trade with me," the other woman offered.

"That's no better!"

Harv said in his sneering, phony drawl, "Red here's okay. Ya just got unseated. We'll go back slow if ya want." She glared, but finally allowed him to toss her up into the saddle.

And go back slow we did. So slow every fly in Ontario found us. Trail rides.

CHAPTER

TWENTY

I handed Harv my dollar-fifty and offered to put Silver in his stall. Harv took the money and grunted. I figured that meant okay. I led the horse, clunking, down the stable aisle. He wanted to turn into a stall so I figured that was his. I took his bridle off, put his halter on and tied him up—on a long rope so he'd have room to move. I took the saddle off.

Harv came by with the chestnut. "Some folks," he muttered. His duck-cut had fallen around his ears. I nodded in agreement.

"Where do I put the saddle?"

"Down there." He gestured vaguely.

I carted it into a messy tack-room, found a

curry comb and a dandy brush. Back in the stall, I started grooming. Silver stood motionless, lower lip ajar, one back hoof cocked. Poor horse, I'll love you. The hard rhythm of grooming in my shoulders, the smoothness of his skin, the smell—in a month, I'd forgotten. How could I have been scared?

Harv led another horse by, another. Then the pretty mare.

"Why don't you turn them out in the pasture?" I asked.

"Can't. Bud says."

When I was brushing Silver's front leg, Harv came back. I could feel him lounging against the stall partition. "Want to see something?" He wasn't drawling as much.

"What?"

"Something."

"Maybe." I moved to Silver's back leg. "What?"

"Something in-*er*-esting." Harv sneered a bit.

"What?" I repeated, brushing Silver's fetlock.

"Have to come see." I looked up. He'd combed his hair back. His brow was arched. My stomach tightened with distrust. I brushed some more. "Why?"

"Because." Harv shifted restlessly against the wooden stall. "Ya do." I waited, brushed. "Yer a good rider," he sort of mumbled.

I shrugged. "If I come back, I want to ride that mare you were riding. What's her name?"

"The Filly. But I dunno if Bud'd let ya. She's a handful."

"I could. What sort of a name's 'filly'? That's just a female horse before she's a mare."

"I dunno. What she's always been called. Ya can't ride her anyways."

"Yeah? Why not?"

" 'Cause. Yer too young. Gonna come 'n see?" His eyebrow was up again.

I figured he was maybe fifteen. Around his pimples he had a blackness as if he were trying to grow a beard. He was pretty dumb. But he was taller than me even if he was skinny, and his faded worn jeans were tight, showing a bulge between his legs. "What should I see?" I stalled.

"Something."

I heaved a sigh and stood up, hefting the brush in my hand. This dumb conversation could go on forever. "If I come back next week, can I ride the Filly?" He shrugged, stuck his thumbs in his belt loops. I stared at him. "You should have told those people how to ride—at least a bit."

"Aw, they're all the same. Want to gallop or fall off. Who cares?"

"The horses do."

He took out his comb, combed, flicked his hair back. "Gonna come 'n see?"

"If I can ride the Filly."

"All right! Come on!"

I put the brush on the stall edge and followed him down the aisle, did a right turn behind him, came to some box stalls.

"So?" I asked, in the dimness.

Harv was grinning at me in a really creepy way. "In there." He jerked his head. I looked.

A horse half asleep, head hanging low, rear hoof at a resting angle. "So?" I said, and then I saw. The horse's penis dangled out a foot and a half, thick and slimy as a knotted kelp strand. At its tip hung a drop of moisture. My stomach churned with anger, embarrassment and—fear, but I wouldn't let Harv know. "So?" I repeated, sneering too.

"Ever seen one that horny? Can't keep it sheathed though he's got no balls." Harv's eyes shone nastily in half-light.

"Sure, I've seen lots of horses." My mouth had gone dry. I tried to swallow.

I turned to leave, but suddenly Harv put his arm out to the stall, blocking my way. "I can get horny, too—wanna see?"

I threw my head up and sniffed in disgust so

my eyes wouldn't go to his crotch out of their own fascination. "Come off it," I sneered, hoping I was glaring too. "Anyway, I gotta go, my mum's expecting me."

"She ain't here."

"Yes, she is. Waiting on the road." I ducked under his arm and walked down the aisle, my back straight. But I could feel him staring.

I continued walking out of the stable, across the yard and down the hill without giving in to my need to run or look back. I was terrified Harv was following, would at any minute grab my arm, whirl me around and show me his horny.

I crossed the road without even looking for cars and, on the other side, glanced back. No one. Then I started to tremble and shake and cry. I could hardly breathe and suddenly had to pee. Where was the bus? I checked my watch, holding my wrist steady with my other hand. Only four-thirty. What if Harv came down the hill and saw me standing here? After what I'd said about Mum? He could really do something—or he could laugh and know I was scared.

I started walking up the road, concentrating on my knees, which wanted to fold backwards. If I got around a bend, I could wait and flag the bus down there. But what if Harv came by? I didn't know where he lived, which way he'd go. What a horrible creep. I was never going back even if it meant not riding until the fall. How dare he! That's what Agatha would say.

Walking stopped my shaking and my knees finally strengthened, but I still had to pee. I ducked into the underbrush, unzipped my jeans, squatted. What if Harv found me now? What were those noises? I didn't have to go. I pulled up my jeans as fast as I could, my underpants in a tangle, and continued walking.

A car. Coming from behind. I cringed and moaned, then ran back into the underbrush, crashing through it until I came to a tree I could hide behind. I closed my eyes and held my breath till the car passed.

I walked on. The hot sun beat down. Horse-flies buzzed around my head like war bombers. I still had to pee and was dying for a drink. I picked up a pebble, rubbed some of the dirt off and sucked it, hoping it would trick my mouth into not being thirsty.

What if something's happened to Agatha while I've been gone? What if she's died? Lying in a crumpled heap on the floor? Or still on her bed? I moaned and shook my arms to get rid of the thought. I should have waited for Lynn to go riding. Harv wouldn't have done that to her. Or if he had, she'd have known what to say. She has brothers.

I must have walked a couple of miles before I heard a honk. I was so scared, I jumped and was about to run back into the woods, but the bus pulled up, just ahead of me. Then I thought: what if Harv takes the bus? I tried to see in the windows, but they were too dusty. I had no choice, except to say I wanted to walk, and I sure didn't. I threw the pebble away, slowly opened the door and climbed in, trying not to look as if I were looking at the passengers. A woman. A child. The driver said, "Thought I'd missed ya. Walked quite a ways."

"Oh—felt like it." I gave him my dime.

I wasn't really sure what horny meant, what a sheath was. Something to do with penises and sex. But what, exactly?

CHAPTER

TWENTY-ONE

I didn't realize I'd fallen asleep until the opening door startled me awake. Mum said, "My goodness, it's so quiet in here. No welcoming committee!" Behind her, Lynn plopped down a heavy suitcase.

I leapt up from the chair, then stumbled. One foot still asleep. I hobbled over, gave Mum's cheek a kiss and grinned at Lynn. "Hi."

"Hi." She grinned back. I felt suddenly shy and wondered if she did too, though probably not. In the nearly a year I'd known her, Lynn was never shy.

Mum said, "Agatha, this is Lynn Hamilton."

Lynn bobbed her head. "How do you do, Miss Adams."

Agatha smiled and her teeth clicked approvingly. "Very well, thank you, Lynn. How do you do?"

I grinned more. I'd told Lynn Agatha likes manners and not to just say hi. "She can call you Agatha, can't she, Agatha?" I picked up Lynn's suitcase. "Come on, I'll show you where we sleep." Before I'd gone riding, I'd hauled another cot down from the attic and made it up, placing it at right angles to mine so our heads would be together.

"Oh, this is fabulous," Lynn declared, looking around the veranda, then out through the screen. Her enthusiasm made me realize how accustomed I'd become to the view. The last of the twilight was royal-blueing the sky. Against it, tree-tops and branches made black patterns. The lake water lapped quietly at the shore. Somewhere nearby a loon lamented. "Let's go swimming," Lynn said.

"Now?"

"Sure." She glanced into the lighted living room; so did I. Mum put some wood into the stove, placed the kettle on, made a comment to Agatha. Lynn leaned closer to me, whispered, "Guess what?"

"What?"

"I'll tell you when we're swimming."

152

Mum has a word for Lynn: *irrepressible*. Nothing can keep Lynn down, nothing can make her unhappy. I guess it's because she has two older brothers and a sister and because of the way she looks: small and slim with sparkly brown eyes and short curly black hair. Her teeth stick out a bit, probably because she sucks her thumb. That's what I noticed first about Lynn, last fall, beginning of Grade Seven. She sat there in her desk and if she were reading or writing, she'd forget where she was and her thumb would go into her mouth. Our teacher, Mr. Preston, would tell her to take it out. She would, with a grin, but five minutes later, back it would go. I admire how brave she is not to be embarrassed. I would be mortified. Even more peculiar, no one teased her. She's really popular.

In our class, when we'd finished our work, we could get a book from the library corner. The first week, both of us reached for the only horse book at the same time. "Oh, do you like horses, too?" she'd asked. "I love them, but no one else in this class does!" Lynn was the only one in the whole class who didn't laugh when we were studying fuels and I said in Vancouver we burned sawdust. We had sawdust burners and sawdust rooms. Mr. Preston didn't believe me and I had to write my uncle for proof, but Lynn did.

"We're going for a swim, Mum," I yelled, then said to Lynn, "Get your bathing suit—mine'll be all clammy, oh well."

"Forget bathing suits. It's dark. Just take your towel. We'll skinny-dip." She grinned while I blinked. It hadn't occurred to me. What if someone saw? But then, swimming at night hadn't occurred to me either. I grinned back.

Mum came to the veranda door. "Swim right by the shore, girls. And don't stay in too long."

We turned our backs to each other while we took off our clothes and wrapped ourselves in our towels. Lynn galloped down the steps and across the sand. Part of me felt irritated because this was my place to show and another part of me wanted to follow her. That part won.

At the edge of the lake, I dropped my towel and crashed in until I was chest high, then dove under. The dark water, warmer than the air, felt silky on my skin. I crawled a few strokes parallel to the shore. I'd never been skinny-dipping before, though I wouldn't tell Lynn that. I thought I knew everything about the feel of water, but—water flowing by all of me, around my chest, my stomach, getting right in between my legs—I stuck my head up and laughed.

Lynn was beside me. Her eyes and the water-rings around her gleamed in the pale lights from the cottage. Mum moved through the window taking tea to Agatha, whose head cut the light as she rocked slowly, back and forth. Everywhere else was dark. Everywhere quiet. Lynn was looking up—millions of stars and, half-bitten by a tree, the crescent moon.

"So—what?"

"What?" Lynn asked back.

"You said 'guess what?' "

"Oh, yeah!" She turned, stroked closer. "It happened. I got it!"

"What?"

"You know—my period. I've been dying to tell you."

I moved the water as if only my arms were swimming, grateful she couldn't see me blushing. All I could think was: you don't look any different. "Should you be swimming?" I asked.

"Silly!" Lynn laughed. "I got it just after you left. It's done now. But I brought a box in case." She sounded pleased with herself.

All I could think now was: Gail's brother works in the drugstore. It's his job to wrap the boxes of pads in plain brown paper and put them on the shelf. "Did you have to go to the store?" I asked. "Did you have to buy some—?"

"At first I didn't. I used my sister's. But then I

did. It wasn't so bad. I got Gail to tell me when Dave wasn't working."

"Clever." I probably sounded admiring. "What did it feel like?"

"At first I didn't feel anything. I just saw the blood. Later it felt a bit gushy."

"Did you have cramps?"

"Nope."

"What did you do?"

"Nothing. I mean, nothing different." We had both started to breast-stroke at the same time, keeping close to the shore. "You don't do anything different, except maybe you don't swim. The pad would get soggy."

In a way, I didn't like this discussion, but in a way I did. Fascinating, but disgusting, like the coloured pictures in Mum's *Home Medical Guide*. "What's the pad feel like?"

"Lumpy. Like something between your legs."

"Ugh." I wished this wasn't going to happen to me. "How long did it last?"

"Four and a half days. But my sister says it'll last longer next time." She still sounded pleased with herself, pleased with it all. I could feel my lip curling. Glad it was dark.

"You're lucky you got it in the summer," I said. "Remember when Louise started at school? She had blood on her skirt and the boys laughed."

"Yeah. But she's always been a twirp." Lynn dripped scorn.

"Well, she didn't plan that to be twirpy." I felt sorry for Louise—not that I wanted to be friends. She was big, older because she'd failed. I was younger because I'd skipped.

"No, but it would happen to someone like her."

Would that happen to me? I paddled around in a circle.

Lynn whispered, "My mum said she used to use rags and she had to wash them every month. Isn't that gruesome?"

"Girls?" Mum, on the veranda. "There's hot chocolate!"

"Coming!" We splashed through the shallow water onto shore, ran for our towels. I peeked at Lynn before she wrapped herself up. Didn't look any different that I could see. She turned, caught me looking. I dropped my gaze, but when I looked up to apologize, she was grinning. "Gail got hers too," Lynn whispered. "But—we're both older than you," she added.

Later, when we were in bed, I told Lynn about Harv and horny. She wanted to go riding the next day so that when Harv showed us his, we could laugh at it. Her sister says that's the best thing to do when boys get stupid about their erections. I guess horny is another word for that.

157

CHAPTER

TWENTY-TWO

When Mum was leaving Sunday night, I realized I hadn't had any time alone with her to ask about my father. We'd found just a few minutes Saturday when Agatha was having her afternoon read and Lynn was outside.

I'd hissed at Mum, "Do you know what? Agatha drinks sour milk! She says she likes it that way! She's crazy! She has it on cornflakes and she has it with that chocolate Quik! It's disgusting, all lumpy and smelly." I made a face and Mum laughed. "She said the storm curdled it, and waste not want not," I continued. "I couldn't stand to watch her! Ugh!"

Mum said something about taste buds being less sensitive in older people or maybe Agatha had to drink it that way as a child, but I still think it's revolting. I told Lynn, and we'll watch to see if she does it this week. If the milk doesn't go sour itself, Lynn says she'll leave it in the sun. But we'll keep some cool for us.

Lynn insisted we go to the stables on Monday. I didn't want to, it was so hot, but Lynn just looked at me through my grumbles with her big brown eyes and expectant smile until I said, "Okay." Was she more interested in seeing Harv than the horses? What if she said something about horny—or laughed? I struggled into my jeans.

"Put this in your pocket." With a funny, embarrassed smile, Lynn held out a white lump.

I took it. "What is it? Why?" A folded-over Kotex pad. "No!" I threw it back. She nearly missed it.

"Don't get it dirty!" She smoothed it, re-folded it. "Please."

"Why?"

"In case. My sister says to be prepared."

"But if you just finished your period, you won't start again for weeks, will you?"

Lynn shrugged. "My sister says it's irregular at first. That means I can get it anytime."

"Well, if you're not having it right now, you won't for a few hours, will you?"

Another shrug. "If I can get it anytime—"

159

"Well, you carry it."

"I don't have any pockets." She smoothed the hips of her red pedal pushers.

"Change your pants."

"Only my shorts have pockets."

"I'll lend you some jeans."

"Just take it. Please." Her voice pleading.

"Oh, good grief." I scrunched up the pad and shoved it in my pocket. An uncomfortable bulge. "It's too big. Someone'll see."

"No, they won't. Anyway, they'll just think it's a handkerchief." Lynn gave me a grin of relief and added, "I probably won't need it."

Oh great. I smacked my tongue on the roof of my mouth. Mum's menstruation lecture didn't cover these practicalities.

With all that, we got to the road just as the bus came along, and a good thing. If it was hot by the lake, it was deadly away from it. There were no other passengers and the driver chatted on about "Hot enough for ya?" and "Goin' to the stables again?" and "Ya up here for the summer, the both of yous?" Finally he let us off.

We were too busy making our legs move up the hot hill to talk. Just about at the top, I stopped and pulled the pad out of my pocket.

Lynn grabbed my arm and snarled, "What are you doing?"

I yanked away, nearly dropping the pad. "Getting the riding money out. I forgot I had it in that pocket. You don't want me fishing around in front of Harv, do you?" I retrieved the money, shoved the pad back in and tried to adjust it semi-comfortably. "It's okay," I said. "There's no one here."

Lynn had moved between me and the top of the hill. She looked around. "Just you wait! You'll find out what it's like to think about it all the time!"

I rolled my eyes. All the time? Lynn almost sounded like her dippy sister.

The closer we got to the stables, the more I wished I hadn't told her about Harv. He might get mean or maybe after she left he'd get back at me. "Lynn? Don't say anything to Harv to let him know I told you?"

"Why not?"

"Because," I said.

"Aw, he's just a boy. We can tease him."

"Don't. Please."

She looked at me quizzically, then shrugged. "Okay. I won't unless he does."

The advantage of the heat was that no one was as stupid as we were to go riding in the middle of the afternoon. The stable yard was deserted. Two horses switched their tails as they lazily grazed in

161

the paddock. We reached the cool of the barn with relief and stood inside, waiting for our eyes to adjust. I could feel someone watching us. Gradually, I made out two shapes—Harv and someone lounging on a bale of hay, watching us.

My heart beat around in my chest. Lynn and I could handle Harv alone, but Harv with a friend? No ride was worth it. I wanted to leave. I could feel Lynn drawing back, too.

"Too hot to ride today," Harv drawled. "Horses're on strike." His friend snorted in approval. Scrawny too, with a long greasy duck-cut, a few pimples. His lips were fuller, though, and his eyes not so slitty. They both chewed on stalks of hay.

"Oh, come off it," Lynn said.

"'Strue, ain't it, Johnny?" Harv winked.

"Sure is." Johnny had attended the same drawl-and-leer school.

"It's not the horses on strike, it's you guys," I said to Harv. "You said I could ride the Filly, remember." I looked around, saw a brown nose sticking over a half-door, a sign above: The Filly. "She looks like she wants to go out."

"Been out twice this morning," Harv grudged. "Besides, Bud ain't here. Gotta ask him."

"You said."

"Did not."

162

"Yes, you did," Lynn butted in. "She told me. You let her ride her or—"

"Or what?" Harv challenged.

"Ohhh—you'll see," she finished.

A long silence, in which Lynn and I stared at the boys, staring at us. I slitted my eyes so they wouldn't blink and gritted my teeth, then trembled with having to stand still; my legs wanted to run me out of there.

"Aw, let 'em ride, Harv," Johnny finally said. "It won't hurt anything."

Harv sighed, threw away his chewed haystalk and got up. "What a job," he said to Johnny, but I knew he was talking to us. "But it is a job. Gimme yer money." He held out his hand. I placed the three dollars in it then nearly blushed: the pad in my other pocket—

"C'n ya ride?" Harv addressed Lynn, defying her to admit it.

"Yes."

"Saddle up Paint, then," he ordered Johnny.

"We can do it," I said. "Show us what saddles and bridles."

But neither paid attention and went about the tasks as if they had glue on the soles of their shoes. I held my breath in case Harv didn't saddle the Filly—but finally, finally, he led her out.

I said thank you, took the reins, adjusted the

163

girth and stirrups, then mounted, all without looking at Harv.

The Filly pricked her ears and pranced. I loved her even more than I thought I would. Lynn was on a large piebald. In spite of his walleye, he didn't look too bad, either. I waited until she was organized, then led the way out of the stable yard.

Under the trees it was cooler. But there was no breeze and all the flies from the last ride lurked in wait. I pulled the Filly over and broke off a leafy branch. She held still until I was ready, then started forward again. I shooed the flies away and patted her neck. Such a lovely horse, she must have some thoroughbred in her and hadn't yet been ruined by trail rides. Or Harv. I grinned over my shoulder at Lynn.

"They weren't so bad," she said. "Just standard-issue creeps. And this is fab. I see what you mean about that horse. She's neat."

Lynn's pad was digging in below my hipbone. I hitched it up higher in my pocket, pulled at my shirt to cover it. "I told you about my friends at home? Scott and Pete?"

"Yeah? So?"

"They're really nice now—or they were up to last year. What if they turn into creepy teenagers? Maybe all boys do?"

Lynn laughed. "Come on, some boys are nice. My brothers aren't so bad—most of the time—and Gail's brother's okay. Creeps like those," she jerked her head back towards the stable, "they were born creeps."

"Yeah, maybe." I was comforted. I only know about Scott and Pete and I'd never thought of them as boys, just—friends who happened to be boys. Then I shook my head. Who wanted to waste time on a horse thinking about boys?

The Filly seemed to want to trot down the slight hill, so I let her. Such a smooth gait, I didn't even have to post. At the bottom of the hill and through the stream, I squeezed her into a canter. Like flying, like riding the wind. She was the horse for me. If I owned her, she'd never be ruined by Harv. Mum could buy her and we'd take her back to Toronto. I'd bike out to the stable every day to see her, no one else would groom her or ride her—

I slowed her to a walk; she might get over-heated. But she was sweating only lightly. How obedient she was; maybe she felt about me as I did about her. We'd never be separated, she couldn't cost too much, not from a stable like this—

"I wish my mum would buy her," I said.

"Would she?"

"She says it's not the cost of the horse, it's the cost of the up-keep." We turned out of the meadow onto the trail leading to the lake.

"You could ask her," Lynn encouraged.

"Mmm. How much do you think she'd cost?"

"I don't know—a hundred dollars? Fifty dollars?"

We trotted along the lake shore, the Filly nimbly avoiding the tree roots that stuck up. I didn't have a hundred dollars, I had only ten. I'd have to find a name, she couldn't be just the Filly. A queen's name? Or Grace—? No! I could never name a horse after her! National Velvet? I loved that book, but Velvet's horse was named The Pie. So why not The Filly? Nope, she had to have a proper name. Velvet something. Velvet Wind? Velvet Steel? Queen Velvet?

I slowed her to a walk and gave her a loose rein, then checked my watch. Time to start up the hill. I turned to tell Lynn—something felt different. I put my hand in my pocket—"The pad's fallen out," I whispered.

"Oh no! Where?" Lynn shrieked and looked around. So did I. No white blob conveniently there. "We have to go back!"

"It's okay," I said doubtfully. "No one'll know it's yours."

"We have to find it! We can't leave it!" Lynn looked more upset than I'd ever known her.

"We can't go back. We don't have enough time!"

"We have to." Lynn tried to turn Paint. He yawed his neck around, but not his body. She kicked him. "Come on!"

"There isn't enough time," I repeated. "Besides, it could be anybody's."

"No, we have to find it! Those guys would know—besides, I might need it! Come on! Please!" The last to Paint as well. He was half-turned, his ears back with stubborn anger. "Harv might think it's yours, you know!"

I spun the Filly and shoved past Paint. He was obviously a follower. "We'll have to be fast then." I hadn't thought about Harv thinking it was my pad, but it was my fault. Maybe it had fallen out along the lake, but more likely when I cantered in the meadow. We'd be late back and I had no money for a longer ride.

We trotted along the trail, keeping our eyes on it for something white. What a long way we'd come, I thought, then I saw it. I pulled the Filly up and yelled, "There!"

But it was a piece of tissue. "Damn," Lynn said.

Both horses were sweating. So were we. I insisted we walk. Back late was better than back with hot horses. Though I wasn't sure Harv or Bud would agree. Finally we turned into the meadow, and the Filly picked up speed, thinking she should canter. But I held her down and re-traced our path through the long grass as well as I could follow it, crushed in all directions. Nothing.

"If we don't see it here, then it's well-hidden," I said. Lynn didn't look comforted. She looked as if she might cry. I was beginning to feel that too.

We crossed through the fence and into the woods. Something at the edge of the stream. The pad. I got down and picked it up. Although only its end was in the water, it had acted like a wick. I held the dripping thing between my thumb and finger and looked at Lynn. She was blinking back tears.

"I'm not putting this in my pocket," I stated.

Lynn's upper teeth held onto her lower lip. She nodded resignedly. "Can you bury it? So no one will find it?"

I scraped between two tree roots with my running shoe, then got a stick and scraped more. In the shallow grave, I placed the soggy pad and pulled dirt back over it with the edge of my shoe. I stepped on it to tamp it down. "That's good," Lynn said.

I had my foot in the stirrup and was just about

to mount when there was a clattering on the trail above us. The Filly neighed and jerked away. I hopped after her, and with more strength than I thought I had, catapulted into the saddle.

Harv and Johnny, doubling bareback on Red. "There ya are! Yer late! Fell off, didn't ya?" Harv accused, joyfully.

"No, I didn't!"

"Yeah, ya did! Knew it!"

"I did not!"

"She did not!" Lynn yelled.

Harv frowned—or sneered more. "What're ya late for then? That's three more bucks. Bud don't allow half hours."

"The horses were hot so we walked," I said.

"Told ya it was too hot. That's three bucks." He yanked Red around and we trekked up the hill behind them. I was thinking how to be reasonable—I'll bring the money next week, we made a mistake with the time, I dropped something, had to find it—

In the stable yard, Harv and Johnny swung off Red. Lynn and I slowly dropped to the ground. Harv looped Red's reins over his arm, whipped his comb out and flicked back his hair. He passed it to Johnny, who did the same. "Three more bucks." Harv half-lowered his eyelids, raised his upper lip and held out his hand.

"We don't have any more money," I said. "Where's Bud? I'll explain it to him." Lynn grabbed my arm and shook it, making a glurpy sound of protest. I wanted to kick her so she'd know I didn't mean the pad but I could only frown.

"Bud's not here, told ya. He's gone fer feed."

"I'll bring the money next time."

Harv withdrew his hand, glanced at Johnny and slimed a smile. "Tell ya what, we'll square it with Bud so ya don't have to pay—fer a kiss."

"Oh, come off it!" Lynn glared. "Someone should tell you what looks good on Elvis looks sick on you! If you think we're kissing you, you're crazy! Come on, Jess, we're going!" She grabbed my arm and propelled me a few yards.

Then she stopped and shouted, "I bet you won't even tell Bud we were here! I bet you'll keep the money for yourselves!"

Johnny yelled something. He and Harv started after us. We turned and ran. At the hill I glanced back. They had three horses to hold onto. In spite of that, Harv was glaring and shaking his fist. Lynn just laughed. In a minute, I did too.

CHAPTER

TWENTY-THREE

Next day we made a container out of oilcloth I found in the attic, some tape for reinforcement and string. We put in three movie magazines, six Dorset bakery cookies wrapped in wax paper, and Lynn's lipstick, mascara and eye shadow. I tied the ends of the string around my neck and we swam to the island. Lynn got there first, even though I'm the faster swimmer. The container dragged at my neck and bobbled on top of the water, hitting me in the face when I took a breath.

"Just one little thing," I panted as I pulled myself up on the rocks, "shouldn't make swimming so hard. You wear it going back."

Lynn untied the string and we climbed up the rock to the top of the island and down the other side. From here we couldn't see the cottage, just the point of land between us and the next bay.

"We can sunbathe nude," Lynn said. "There's no one to see."

"You can. I'm not," I declared firmly. Skinny-dipping at night was one thing, but lying about in the daytime—

"Oh, well, if you're not—" Lynn rummaged in the container. The corners of the magazines were a little soggy, but the cookies were fine. She took one, passed them to me. Oatmeal with raisins. I had one, then another.

"This is the life." Lynn lay down on her back, arms behind her head. Beads of water trickled through the fine hairs on her forearm. My sun-drying skin prickled, but not uncomfortably. I lay down too, closed my eyes.

"Did you know Harv and Johnny wouldn't give Bud the money, or did you guess?"

"Guessed," she murmured, "but I was pretty sure. They're such creeps."

"Fancy kissing them."

"Yeah. Ugh. No sex appeal. Not like Marlon. Or Elvis. They have S.A."

"I hate kissing," I said.

"Yeah. It's okay in the movies, though. Watching it, I mean." We both laughed. Lynn leapt up and I opened my eyes. She fished her lipstick out of the oilcloth. "My sister's working at the Five and Dime this summer. She got me this. Passion Perfect." She stretched her lips, dabbed at them, rubbed them together. "How's it look?"

"Really red. Why not Perfect Passion?" I giggled. Names of lipsticks are so silly. Lynn and Gail aren't allowed to wear lipstick so every school morning they put it on at my house. Sometimes I wear it with them, but I don't like the feel.

Lynn was putting on the eyeshadow. "It's hard to do without a mirror."

"Let me," I offered.

"It's okay." She unscrewed the mascara, blinked her eyelashes fast against the brush. "How's that?"

"You got a blob on your cheek." She wiped it off, then fluttered her lashes and pursed her red lips in my direction. "Dahling, I love you. I can't live without you." Kiss, kiss.

"Oh yetch!" I stuck out my tongue and held my stomach. She laughed with me. I lay down again and closed my eyes.

"Let me do you," Lynn said.

"All right, if you make me look like Grace Kelly." Her fingers tickled gently as she rubbed on the eyeshadow. I held very still so she wouldn't poke my eye out with the mascara, then stretched my lips for the lipstick. "Not too much," I muttered.

"You're not really pretty, but with the right make-up you could be cute." Lynn's tone was serious; I'd been joking about looking like Grace Kelly. She continued, "You've got a good personality and that shows through. My sister says you can put make-up on to heighten the personality."

I lay completely still. It's one thing to *think* you're not pretty, and another to have your friend tell you you're not.

"I hope I didn't hurt your feelings." Lynn's tone was anxious. I shrugged. "I said you have a good personality—that's the most important—"

"Don't say your sister says! Call her by her name! It's not a secret. I know it's Martha."

So my feelings are hurt. Stinging. Lynn's not that pretty either. Her teeth stick out. Even Martha's not that pretty—she has a fat rump.

I sat up, hugged my knees. "Handsome is as handsome does, Agatha says. She says she was pretty once and look at her now. It's not important." Except if you're Grace Kelly.

"You're right," Lynn soothed. "I like the way you look. Interesting." I sighed loudly and glared. "And you're prettier with make-up."

"Oh, have a cookie!" I threw it at her and dove into the water.

When I stuck my head up, Lynn looked close to tears. "I'm sorry," she mumbled.

"Forget it, okay?" I swam around for a few minutes then hauled myself up onto the hot rocks again. "Is it smear-proof make-up?" I grinned.

"Not bad. At least the Passion Perfect." She grinned too. We both lay down on our stomachs. I could smell the dry, dusty heat of the rock. A bug crawled across it. I stuck my finger out. It waved its feelers at it, then detoured.

"So what's Agatha like?" Lynn asked. "Is she bossy?"

"Not much. She was at first, but mainly she just reads and putters. She seems all right—"

"What do you mean?"

I shrugged. "Oh—you know—she's old—"

"Mm. My gran died when I was in Grade Five. She was eighty."

"Agatha's seventy-five."

"Oh, well then." Lynn sounded as if Agatha'd live another five years.

"My father was sixty-three."

"What'd he die of?"

I paused, not knowing what to say. "Heart failure."

175

"Oh yeah? Same as my gran."

"Agatha was friends with my father's sister, Mary, who I'm named after—"

"Your Aunt Mary."

"She can't be my Aunt Mary because she died before I was born. Can she?"

Lynn considered, finally shrugged. "I don't know. Everybody of mine is alive—except my gran."

"Was your father in the war?" I asked.

"No. He wanted to be but he worked at the airport so they made him stay there."

"Mine was in World War One."

"I know, you told me."

"I didn't tell you this. He was here, staying with Agatha for two weeks once, when he wasn't much older than us!"

"Yeah? Really? When?" Lynn propped herself on her elbows, looking at me.

"I guess it would have been about 1900."

"Wow, that long ago! That's neat! How come he was so old when you were born?"

"I don't know."

"Maybe he was waiting for your mum," Lynn laughed. "True love. But how come she married someone so much older?"

"Mum says the generations got mixed up because so many men were killed." It's true, I thought, most of Mum's friends didn't get married or are widows like her. I added, "Love doesn't have anything to do with age, Mum says."

"That's really romantic. It's too bad he died. They weren't married for long."

"Ten years."

"But he was sick for years you said—what with? A disease?"

"I don't know."

"Mmm. My parents are having their twentieth anniversary in November."

I could hardly hear Lynn. I'd never thought of Mum falling in love like the movies and getting married. Having a honeymoon. She's always been Mum. And my father? Was he romantic before he got sick?

Lynn was staring at me as if I looked funny. I searched for something, anything to say.

"There's this book I'm reading." I rolled onto my side and propped my head on my hand. "*Amarylis*. There's this fourteen-year-old boy who falls in love with this five-year-old girl—" That's closer in age than my parents. I closed my eyes and sighed, then "—he promises to wait for her forever—they're always saying," I put on a baby voice, " 'Do you weawy wuv me, John Guido? Weawy?' " changed it to a bass, " 'Yes, my darling Amarylis, I really love you, you are so beautiful with your golden ringlets and your rosebud lips'—"

Lynn was rolling around on the rock, clutching her stomach in laughter. I started to giggle, too. "They do nothing but talk in the book, and look at flowers, even the five-year-old never gets dirty or angry, and John sounds ninety-three at least."

"Can you imagine!" Lynn chortled.

"It's so soppy! He even kisses her, and strokes her hair, and she promises to marry him!"

"At five? How icky!"

"Her handsome—she's always calling him handsome—John Guido!"

"You're making it up!"

"I am not! I'll show you the book!"

"Oh, come on!" Lynn crashed into the water with a loud splash. She came up spluttering and feebly pulled herself back onto the island. "That's so funny! Did they really talk soppy like that then?"

"I guess so." I remembered Mary's inscription in the Emily Dickinson book she gave to Agatha.

"I was thinking of Harv," Lynn said, in a minute. "Can you imagine!" She started to laugh again, but not as wildly.

"No, I can't! That gives me the creeps! This guy's nice, at least. Stupid, but nice. Here, let's read." I tossed her a magazine, took one myself. We'd read all of them at least five times, but I liked looking at the pictures. And it was quiet.

Only for a minute. Lynn waved hers in front of me. "See this?"

A still shot from *On the Waterfront*. Marlon Brando lounging against a door in his T-shirt, Eva Marie Saint half-turned away, wearing a slip. The small picture on the next page was of them kissing. "I know he's your heart-throb. So?"

"We should practise kissing so we're ready."

I rolled over. "What?" She was looking serious. "Ready for what?"

"Kissing's an art, my sis—Martha says. We should practise. Have you?"

"What?"

"Practised kissing?"

"No." A lie. Last spring I kissed a picture of my father in his uniform. One of the times I was wearing Lynn's lipstick. Half my father covered in a red smudge, and I couldn't get it off. Mortified. I hid the picture in my bottom drawer. I'd never tell anyone. "No," I repeated. "Have you?"

"Well—at the mirror. My pillow. But Martha says the first time she got kissed she wrecked it because she didn't know what to do. Where to put her nose and that stuff. Like, do you close your eyes?"

"They do in the movies. Who kissed her?"

"She said not to tell."

"I won't."

"Fred Spence."

"Ugh. Who'd want to practise for him?"

"For someone you like." Lynn gave me a look I couldn't place. She leaned closer. More eyeshadow on her left than her right lid. Beads of lake—or sweat—on her forehead. "Look at movie stars. They have to kiss all sorts of people. They have to know how to do it."

"They go to acting school," I said automatically. But I'd never thought of it. Were there kissing classes in acting school? Did Grace Kelly have to learn to kiss? I shrugged. "So, how do we practise?"

"With each other."

"With—? You're crazy!" I slithered up the rock until I was higher than her. "I hate kissing! Especially on the mouth! My uncle used to kiss on the mouth! His moustache tickled!"

"I don't have a moustache. Practise for people without moustaches."

"I thought you meant practise at the same time. Why don't we each kiss our hands?" I did it—quickly smacked the back of my hand.

"Won't work. Hands don't kiss back."

Then I remembered Lynn's look. In science

180

we'd had to do a project on the new St. Lawrence Seaway. We all had ideas, but Lynn had objections to any ideas but hers. A look that brooked no opposition—I'd read it somewhere.

Still, I tried. "Kissing comes naturally when you want to. Maybe your sister didn't want to kiss Fred. I wouldn't."

Lynn gave me her look of scorn. I glanced longingly at the lake, blue, sparkling, cool, and gave in. "Oh well, just for a minute. But rub some of that lipstick off."

Lynn smeared her arm across her lips, rubbed her lips together and swallowed. She inched closer to me. Licked her lips. I licked mine too, wiped my mouth with my hand. Her face was awfully close. I shut my eyes; might as well go for the total experience. All for stage and screen.

Contact. I drew back. Opened my eyes. Lynn was frowning. "That wasn't a kiss!"

"Yes, it was. Your lips touched mine."

"A baby kiss. Not a real kiss."

I closed my eyes again. Lynn's lips stayed against mine. Cool at first, then warm. They moved. I drew back, looked at her.

"You're not getting into it," she stated. "Think of Grace Kelly and—um—"

"Gary Cooper? Who are you thinking of?" As if I didn't know.

"Marrrr-lon." Lynn nearly swooned in ecstasy. This time she put her arm around my shoulder so I couldn't move away.

I thought of Grace Kelly and Gary Cooper in *High Noon*. I thought of Grace Kelly and James Stewart in *Rear Window*. I leaned into the kiss and moved my lips a bit. Then I jerked away.

"What?" Lynn blinked.

"I just thought of Harv."

"Well, don't. Think of who you want to kiss. We're doing okay with noses, aren't we?"

"Oh—fine. They haven't been a problem."

"We should stand up and practise—like how Clark Gable lurches into Vivien Leigh in *Gone With the Wind*. The bend-over-backwards stuff. I'll show you."

"Agatha might see."

"Well, kneel then."

Bits of rock dug into my knees. Lynn came at me with a ferocious expression. She threw her left arm around my shoulder and her right around my waist. I toppled over with her on top. "Ow!" I shoved her off and untangled my leg. Then I started to laugh.

"Stop laughing," she laughed. "We still have to practise the little flirty kisses and the heavy breathing."

"Heavy breathing? Who heavy breathes?"

"In confession stories they always do."

"Oh, Lynn!" I grabbed her and kissed her. Warmly and firmly. I let my lips move as they wanted to. They felt her teeth. My tongue kissed her teeth. My breath breathed into hers. Then I pushed her away and dove into the water. Where I had a reason to breathe heavily—after two times around the island.

When I pulled myself out again, Lynn had re-lipsticked so thickly her lips almost glowed. "Well, dahling," she lah-di-dahed with arched eyebrows, "wouldn't you say we're experts now? Who do you want to kiss first?" She bit into a cookie with her teeth bared so the lipstick wouldn't smear.

I shrugged, looked at the lake, ran my fingers through my hair and shook the drops off. They made instant black blotches on the rock, then sizzled away. I wished my buzzing confusion would do the same. I didn't think I had a first kiss left.

CHAPTER

TWENTY-FOUR

At lunch Agatha sniffed. "You've been painting, I see. If ladies must use make-up, it shouldn't be obvious. Art, not artifice." It was her first "lady" comment in over a week.

Lynn said, "We've been practising. For when we're famous movie stars." She laughed.

I looked intently at my egg sandwich and willed myself not to blush. *Practising*?

We ate in silence for a few bites, then Agatha announced, "The family next door had a son who went into pictures before the last war. The Tones. Their son, Franchot—"

"Franchot Tone?" I interrupted. "He lived next door?"

"Yes. They summered here. Americans. Franchot moved to Hollywood in nineteen-twenty-something or thirty. Involved in a disgraceful brawl not long ago over an actress. And to think, he was brought up to be a gentleman!" Agatha shook her head.

"I've seen him! Haven't you, Lynn? I can't remember in what, but I have!"

"Sure! Sort of a Fred Astaire type—?"

"Right! He lived in the next cottage? And you never told me, Agatha!"

"I didn't think of it. No one's been up for at least ten years. The cottage is sadly in need of repair—"

I looked at Lynn, she looked at me, and we were thinking the same thing.

As soon as was polite, we excused ourselves, put our dishes in the sink and sauntered out the back door. Then we ran. The bush was so thick and overgrown between the cottages we had to work our way nearly to the lake before we could get through.

The cottage is similar to Agatha's—a stone base and rough boards above, a long veranda—but placed differently on the property so it looks towards the other side of the island. It's definitely dilapidated—thick moss on the roof and brambles growing in and out of loose boards. I'd been over here the first week and hadn't found anything interesting, but now—

We climbed up on the veranda and peered through a crack where the shutters didn't meet.

"Just think, a real movie star lived here! I can't believe it!" I was whispering. "All the time I've been next door and haven't known! What if Grace Kelly'd lived here?"

"Or Marlon," Lynn breathed. "Or Elvis." She hummed the first bars of "Heartbreak Hotel."

"He'd be too noisy." I couldn't see much: some dark shapes that might be furniture.

Lynn nudged me so she could peer in. "Are the doors locked?" She rattled the knob, twisted it. Old-fashioned and rusty, but solid. The shutters met tightly over the other window.

We walked around the side of the cottage, through brambles and bird droppings. By stretching, I could just touch the window ledges. Lynn couldn't.

The back door had a hasp and padlock, again rusted, again solid. I stepped back and looked up to the second storey while Lynn fiddled with the lock. "He slept up there probably—do you think he knew he was going to be a movie star?"

I'm sorry to disappoint you, Father. I cannot follow your footsteps into business. I must leave for Hollywood at once—

186

"Do you think he was here when my father was? Do you think they knew each other?"

Come to Hollywood with me, Robert—

"Hey, these screws are loose!" Lynn was twisting and pulling at the part joined to the door frame. "Get a screwdriver!"

"How? Agatha'd ask what we need it for. Do you think Agatha had them to dinner?"

"Imagine inviting a movie star for dinner. 'You can sit beside me, Marlon'," Lynn phony-swooned, the back of one hand to her forehead. " 'I hope you like pheasant-under-glass.'" Her tone changed. "Do you remember what he looks like?"

"Who?"

"Franchot Tone, of course."

"Well—like Fred Astaire? That's what you said. I'm not really sure I've seen one of his movies. Have you?"

"Oh—what's the diff? He's a movie star." She pulled at the hasp, twisted it.

"Hey," I remembered, "there's an old nail file in the outhouse!"

I ran back to get it. Guess who was coming out? "Ah, there you are, Jessica. I recall it was quite a nasty affair. Another actor beat Franchot up very badly. They both wanted the same actress, but I believe Franchot married her when he got out of the hospital. Of course, these Hollywood marriages—" More head-shaking. "I believe this was his third or fourth—and it didn't last. Hollywood is morally corrupt." Agatha smiled, patted my arm. "Now I'm going to have a little read, my dear. It's good you have a friend to play with. An old lady like me isn't much company."

"Yes, you are, Agatha, you're good company." I smiled the warmth I was feeling for her.

"Well then," she muttered, and "My, my," but she took my arm so I could escort her to the steps.

"Was he here when my father was? Did they know each other?"

"Gracious, no! Franchot's much younger! Why, he can't be more than fifty now!"

"Oh. Have a good read," I said, going back to the outhouse. The nail file must have been there since the turn of the century—if they had nail files then. But it was solid.

I handed it to Lynn. "Mum says there isn't a job that a nail file or bobby pin can't do." I watched the movements of her hands. "Agatha just said Franchot Tone's really young, only fifty." We both laughed. "She also said he married the actress after he got out of hospital. I wonder who she was."

"Grace Kelly! She has a secret marriage in her sordid past!"

188

"Oh, come off it!" I yelled and Lynn laughed. She turned back to the nail file. "Is it working?"

"Mmm. Fits." Concentrating.

Minutes. I asked, "How's it going?"

"The screws're rusty—one's turning—and the other, just a sec—there!" She pulled back the metal piece complete with hasp and padlock. She triumphantly pushed open the door, then looked at me. "You go in first. It's your house—in a way."

"No, you did the work." We were being more polite than scared, though it smelled awfully old and musty.

"Together?" That wasn't possible. The door had swollen in its jamb and we had to squeeze through sideways. Lynn went first. I yanked at the door so we could have more light. It scraped along the floor with a high-pitched whine. "Shhh," Lynn hissed.

I knew what she meant: even though the closest person was Agatha, who was asleep and if not, partly deaf, we still didn't want to disturb anyone. "Ghosts," I giggled. It felt as if there had been people in this room; they'd left only moments before. Spooky, but not menacing. "Don't tell me any horror movies you've seen, okay?"

"Wouldn't think of it," Lynn agreed. Then, "Did you ever see the one with—?

189

"No!" I punched her arm.

"Kidding," she laughed.

I'd been staring at the pump beside the tin sink as my eyes adjusted to the gloom. Now I looked around. Pale yellow cupboards, a blackened wood stove, a table covered in oilcloth against a wall. A big room. Chairs around the table, in the corners. I moved past Lynn, into the doorway to the front room.

The feeling of just-vanished people grew stronger. Women in gauzy dresses to their knees and cloches on their heads. Men with slicked-back hair and boaters. They drank cocktails—did they invite Agatha? The children had a nanny who sat in a canvas chair while they played by the lake. They wore white shorts and dresses—or was I mixing up the illustrations in *Amarylis*? Such a strong impression. I rubbed the goose-bumps on my arms. But I knew the people didn't mind our being here. They seemed to be laughing gently.

I walked in. A large table, a small one, chesterfield and some chairs, with dustcovers. "Dusty covers," I said. My voice sounded normal. Echoed normally.

"Yeah." Lynn was staring at a large empty floor space.

"That's where they had the piano." I knew it for a fact.

"Yeah? Maybe he was in musicals. Let's go upstairs."

The same sort of wide stairs against the wall as at Agatha's. Probably the same person built both houses. But this storey had been finished. Four doors faced a wide landing. It was almost totally dark—only a little dimness behind us. Lynn said, "Maybe we should get a flashlight."

I held onto her wrist and stretched to open the nearest door. Cracks of strong sunlight filtered through the shutters and lit up dust motes set to dancing by our disturbance. A double bed covered with a counterpane, a dresser, a rag rug. We opened the next door: a smaller room with a single bed stripped to its striped mattress. Under it, half-protruding, a chamber pot. The third room was similar.

"Which one do you think was his?" asked Lynn.

"I don't know. The first was probably the parents'."

I turned the fourth knob. The door stuck; I shoved. It squeaked open grudgingly. I stepped across the threshold—

Rustlings, boomings, clattering. My whole body

curled in on itself. I screamed and clutched Lynn's wrist. She pulled me away so hard I staggered.

Something reaching for me from behind— long bony fingers. I could feel their tickling brush on the back of my neck. We bolted down the stairs, through the kitchen and out the door. We didn't stop until we got to the edge of the lake.

"What was that?" Lynn gasped. Her eyes were enormous, her face white.

"I don't know! I've never heard anything like it!" Dead bodies rattling chains, a blood-sucking vampire? I was shivering in spite of the sun. I clutched my chest; pain—was it heart failure?

"We left the door open! It could come after us!" Lynn gave the house a fearful glance.

"I'm not going back!" I whispered. We listened hard: silence. The lake lapped gently near our feet. Leaves rustled. We jumped, looked at each other.

"Just the breeze," Lynn said. "The house looks innocent." It did, but what horrible beast lurked in it? A ghost? Mad at being disturbed? My father's ghost, after me? I shook myself to get that thought away. If it were supernatural, what good would locking the door do? If it weren't, it could have got out already.

"I suppose we should lock the door," I faltered, hoping Lynn would disagree. "At least close it."

She looked at me. Some colour was returning to her cheeks. I took a deep breath—perhaps not heart failure, though my legs still trembled. "If we have to." Lynn sounded dubious. "If we both go."

We again glanced at the cottage, again listened. "There's no such thing as ghosts," Lynn stated, as if convincing her eyebrows, up in denial. I just blinked, swallowed, tried to steady my knees, my heart. "Is there?" she added more firmly.

I didn't want to say, "There might be." Didn't want to say, "Maybe in that house." So I shook my head in agreement.

Down here by the lake, in the sunshine, it didn't make sense to be scared. We both looked over to Agatha's cottage. Her bedroom window faced this way; she was sleeping right there. At the same time, Lynn and I noticed we were still holding hands. We let go. And tried to smile.

"Better than a horror movie," Lynn said. "Girls attacked in abandoned cottage." But her voice still shook. "Do we have to go back to close the door?"

I nodded. I didn't want to but I knew I'd worry about it. I hate open doors. Anything can get out. Or in.

"Okay," Lynn said, but she stayed close behind me as we tiptoed around the side of the house. I stopped at the corner and peeked towards the back door. No thumpings, no chains rattling. An innocent pattern of sun and shadow flickered on the stoop. "Do you still have the screws?" I whispered.

Lynn pulled them out of her pocket as we gingerly and quietly tiptoed up the steps. My heart started battering again. I closed my eyes as I pulled the door shut. Then I gave her the nail file. She got the hinge screwed back into the wood in record time, considering how her hands were trembling. I had to keep looking over my shoulder and try not to say, "Hurry up."

"Done," she whispered. We both ran back to the lake fast. "What do you think it was?" Lynn asked again.

"I don't know. A ghost?" She sort of sneered. I tried to laugh. "Casper, the Friendly Ghost?"

"No, The Mummy."

"Ugh! Don't say that!"

Lynn deepened her voice. "Marley. The Ghost of Christmas Past." She stalked at me. I shook my head, trying to smile, but I put my hands out in front and backed up. "Dracula. House of Wax." My stomach was tickling. Her voice boomed through the buzzing in my ears. "Vincent Price in *The Pit and the Pendulum*." She was thundering now. "*The Murders in the Rue Morgue*. Bodies rising up from open graves, dripping gore." She grabbed my arm.

"Stop!" I was shaking, practically breathless. "Witch Hazel, from Little Lulu."

"Witch Hazel? She's not scary. She's funny! She inks in the holes in her black stockings!"

"So? Let's laugh, ha ha." Lynn gave me the look you'd give a baby when you don't know what it's doing. But I didn't care. "Let's get our bathing suits on," I said.

We went for a swim and then lay in the sun.

TWENTY-FIVE

I hadn't swum away my fear. It came back as we lay in the sun. Bony hands raking lightly over my back. I told myself the tickling was beads of water drying on my thighs. Still, I had to sit up to be sure. I wished I could go to my cave. But it wouldn't be polite to leave Lynn. Or she'd ask where I was going and find my cave. I wiggled my towel around so I could look at the trees protecting it.

"I know what," Lynn interrupted. "Let's tape initials of boys we love on our arms. We'll leave the tape on all summer and the initials will be permanent for school."

"I don't love any boy. Neither do you," I muttered, hoping that would stop her.

"Well, movie stars then." I should remember, nothing stops Lynn. She ran up to the cottage, returned with adhesive tape and scissors. She cut a large MB, taped it on her forearm and held it out. "There. What do you think?" Fine black hairs on her arm.

I think it's dumb. I didn't say it. I took the tape and cut out GK—

"Oh, come on! Has to be a male movie star!"

"Who says?"

"Everyone. It has to be. Take Gary Cooper, at least."

"It's my arm." I taped it on and lay down. Lynn made a disgusted noise. She cut out E, L, V, I, S, stuck them on her thigh and lay down too. Soon my skin was pricking—the exchange of drying lake water for sweat.

"When you were little," I found myself saying, "did anyone tickle you?"

"What?" Lynn's voice drowsy.

I found myself repeating myself.

"What do you mean?"

"What I said."

"Sure."

"Who?"

"Oh—my brothers."

"Your father?"

"Sure, I guess so."

"What did you do?"

"I don't know. Tickled them back. Why?"

I wanted to stop asking, but I couldn't. "No reason. Did you mind?"

I felt Lynn roll over, probaby looking at me. I closed my eyes more tightly. "I've never told anyone this, so don't you—" her tone was hushed and my stomach closed up "—but we still do— tickle each other, all of us down on the floor, my brothers and sister and me, we roll around and tickle until we almost cry, it's fun."

Fun? My stomach was hurting. I didn't know what to say so I said, "I won't tell."

Lynn leaned closer. "Don't you like being tickled?" Moth marks on my stomach. "Kitchee, kitchee—"

I leapt right up and screamed, "Don't you ever do that again!" I could have kicked her and stamped on her and pounded her. I ran into the lake and screamed in a mouthful of water, came up choking, coughing. Lynn was there, thumping my back.

"Gee, I'm sorry, Jess."

Don't touch me! I couldn't say it for choking.

She kept on thumping. I gasped. She put her arm around my waist and helped me to shore.

When I could see again, her huge brown eyes were staring at me. "You scared me," she said.

"Sorry."

"What did you act like that for? I wasn't going to hurt you." She sounded a bit mad. I could only shrug. She added, "I sure won't touch you if that's what's going to happen."

I nodded automatically. My stomach, my whole skin, my feet, were tickling. I nodded again, felt full of nodding, took some deep breaths and tottered to my feet. I made myself look at the lake, the cottage, the bright blue sky. I shivered, picked up my towel and wrapped it around my shoulders. Goose-bumps prickled on my arms. The bottom corner of K had come unstuck. I tried to paste it down, but it curled up again. "Need new tape," I said, to Lynn's foot. I glanced at her face. Didn't know what I saw. Worry? Fear? Anger? I laughed. "Hand me the tape."

I went to the outhouse, then passed through the cottage for my book. As I was picking it up, Agatha opened her bedroom door, sleepy from her afternoon read. I tried to smile and she did, too. She never talks till she's been up half an hour.

I rejoined Lynn on our towels in the sun. I didn't want to think about anything so I read the soppiest, silliest bits of *Amarylis* aloud. Lynn rolled around hysterically and I started giggling so I couldn't get the words out properly. Which made us laugh even more. Finally Agatha came onto the veranda and said she was too old to deal with sunstroke, did we want to be the death of her?

"Let's make dinner," Lynn said to me, "as a treat for Agatha."

Agatha said, "You don't have to," and, "It's all right, I like cooking," but we insisted.

Lynn made macaroni and cheese out of a package and I grated carrots onto lettuce leaves and surrounded them with tomato wedges. On top I put a dollop of mayonnaise.

"It's a very fine dinner," Agatha said, when she'd finished everything.

Then, with a giggly glance at me, Lynn handed her the glass of milk she'd left for two days in the sun. It had a scum on top, and curdles down its sides. Lumpy and slimy—like the things my father ate—eggnogs and custard and soft-boiled eggs all mushed in a cup—

I started clearing the table so I wouldn't gag.

"How very kind of you," Agatha exclaimed. She took a large drink then wiped her moustache with a serviette.

—Mum fed him with a spoon—

"You really do like it, don't you?" Lynn stated.

"Oh, yes. Though I like it even better with that chocolate powder."

—Why hadn't he eaten proper food?

"When did you start drinking sour milk?" Lynn asked. "As a child?"

—Why had he had to be fed like a baby?

"No, no. Not until I started coming here. It's a legacy of no ice-box. The cooler, as you know, doesn't always work when it's very hot."

Lynn looked at me and whirled her finger "crazy" by her forehead. Agatha laughed and finished her milk. I made myself smile. Then Lynn and I did the dishes, and we all played Monopoly until bedtime. No one won.

Loud thumps and bangings and an ominous rustling wakened me. Someone dragging something across the attic—I pulled the covers to my chin and lay as still as possible, trying not to breathe, not to think, sure the beating of my heart would direct him here. A hand touched me. I screamed.

Lynn. A frantic whisper. "Did you hear that? It's the same sound as—"

I nodded. Too terrified to speak. More thumps, whooshings, a bang, directly above our heads.

Lynn clutched me more tightly. "It's Vincent

201

Price. Dracula. The House of Wax. What'll we do?"

"I don't know!" There was nothing I could do. I was frozen to the bed, even though I was sticky with sweat. My breath caught in my throat, making me gag. I wished we were sleeping inside; the screening on three sides suddenly felt very fragile.

Lynn let go of me, rummaged around, switched on her flashlight. "Turn it off!" I hissed. "It'll direct him to us faster!"

"If it's a ghost, it won't make any difference." But she switched it off. The dark looked darker then. I strained my eyes. "Oh!" I remembered and felt really dumb. "Flying squirrels!"

A light glowed inside somewhere, pale, bobbing—

"Girls?" Agatha's voice. "Are you all right? Do you need anything?"

"Sorry, Agatha. I forgot about the flying squirrels."

"What?" Lynn half-sat up.

I took a gigantic breath, let it out, telling my heart to calm down. "Flying squirrels. That's what it was this afternoon, too."

Lynn flopped back on her pillow and laughed. "Was I scared! Every horror movie I've seen! Good thing you know what the problem is."

CHAPTER

TWENTY-SIX

The days rolled hot and sunny into each other. Lynn cut her finger on the bread knife so she wore more adhesive tape. We picked at the corners of our initials to see if we could see the difference even though we knew it was too soon.

One evening at dusk we went upstairs with flashlights to try to surprise the flying squirrels. From the noise they made, I expected them to be as huge as bears. But they're cute little things with large eyes and loose flaps of skin between their legs.

We found pieces of birch bark and tried to make canoes like the kind you see in stores with Ontario or Canada printed on them. But we couldn't get the bark to bend; it broke, even when we soaked it in the lake. So we pencilled messages on the bark's white side. Lynn wrote Marlon, I love you, forever yours, Lynn. Too soppy, I thought. I just drew a heart and put GK and JC in it. We launched those pieces into the lake and watched them bob away on the waves. Then we wrote other messages: Help! I'm being held captive in a haunted cottage; Murderer at large, phone Police; Do not turn upside down—shrunken people on board.

On Friday we baked a cake—with sour milk—to welcome Mum. It came out of the oven lopsided. Agatha said it takes practice to bake in a wood stove. We filled the lop side with chocolate icing and Agatha said you couldn't tell by looking. Then we wondered if it tasted right. By the time Mum arrived about nine, half the cake was gone.

After I'd kissed Mum and she'd greeted Agatha and Lynn, we had tea and the rest of the cake. Mum said it was delicious and had another piece. Then she exclaimed, "Oh, I nearly forgot!"

She crossed to her suitcase and picked up the newspaper she'd placed on top. "I saved this for you, Jess."

I unfolded the paper. Headlines jumped up at me. Lynn leaned over to read too.

Grace To Marry Prince

Grace Kelly today announced her engagement to Prince Rainier of Monaco and her retirement from motion pictures. The radiant princess of screen stated, "I have never been happier." Monaco is a small principality off the south of France, mainly known for its gambling capital, Monte Carlo.

I let the paper drop. Lynn grabbed it, continued reading. I stood up. My chair crashed over. I yanked it up and thumped it into the table so hard the teacups rattled. "How can she do this to me!" I shouted.

"It's so romantic," Lynn exclaimed. "A real prince!"

"Romantic! It's awful! Look at him! He's shorter than she is and going bald—"

"Appearance isn't everything," Agatha interjected, but I cut her off with a glare.

"How can she marry anyone? She has to keep making movies!" I ran out through the veranda and down to the lake. The door slammed behind me. I wanted to scream, to hit someone. I tore her adhesive tape initials off my arm, glad and mad the hairs smarted underneath. I scrunched the tape into a ball and pounded that fist into my other hand. She's left me! I'm all alone! No one to talk to! She doesn't care about me! Said she did, said we're best friends! No one to talk to about my father! How could she leave me? Tears burned the rims of my eyes, blurred the lake—

"I didn't know you'd take it this way, dear." Mum. I hadn't heard her approach. "You read everything about her so I thought—"

"It's not your fault," I mumbled. "It's just—oh, how could she!" I stuffed the tape into my pocket, then leaned against Mum and sobbed. She patted my back. I felt as if I'd lost a part of my life.

When I could speak again, I said, "I don't mind her getting married much, it's quitting movies! She could do both, couldn't she? Couldn't she?"

"You mean work and be married, too? Yes, but maybe she doesn't want to work any more. And a prince—" Mum paused. The lake lapped gently right by our feet. I shifted and sniffed. Keeping one arm around my shoulder, Mum handed me a tissue. "Maybe he insists she not make movies. A prince has responsibilities. Maybe he wants her to help him. Maybe being princess of Monaco will be a full-time job."

"Oh, maybe, maybe," I muttered. None of it helped the tearing hole inside me. I felt as if I'd

206

been promised something and I'd counted on it and now it was gone.

"Maybe," Mum's voice lightened, "she won't retire from movies. Maybe she'll change her mind. How about that maybe?" She squeezed my shoulder, trying to be reassuring.

"Oh, maybe." But I knew that, even if Grace Kelly did make another movie, it wouldn't be the same. I'd never talk to her again.

In the morning I woke up to a word in my head: betrayed. Grace Kelly had betrayed me. Marrying someone. Leaving movies. Leaving ME. And Lynn didn't understand. She chattered on about how romantic it was for a beautiful, blond movie star to be marrying a prince—just like a fairy tale. Nobody understood. It wasn't important to Mum or to Agatha. Though Mum kept sending me question hooks: Why was I taking it so hard? Even I didn't understand why I felt so awful— and I was mad I felt this way.

We went to Huntsville to do the weekly shopping. I tried to not read the headlines in the papers, but my eyes wouldn't obey me. "Yes, I am definitely retiring from pictures," one quoted her as saying. I wanted to chuck the stack of newspapers into the dusty gutter, watch her face blow down the main street of Huntsville, slamming into every telephone pole. But all I had to throw were the balled-up bits of adhesive tape I'd stuffed in my pocket.

Mum asked, "Would you like to have a soda?"

"Yes, please," Lynn said eagerly.

"I don't care," I grumbled. "I'm not hungry." But I finished it.

Lynn spent the whole weekend trying to make me feel better. I just felt worse—mad at myself for not feeling better, mad at myself for causing someone to try to make me feel better, mad at myself for not being a better hostess. The more Lynn tried, the more I tried; finally even our attempts at smiles were as lopsided as the cake.

Her sucking her thumb while she read drove me crazy. Baby, I thought, then hated thinking that. Sorry, I thought, I know you're not. We read most of Sunday, Lynn on the veranda and I in the living room, except for the few hours it took to have lunch at Port Cunnington.

When it was time for Mum and Lynn to leave, I was glad to see her go. I wanted to think in peace about how I was feeling. I didn't want Mum to go in the same way I wanted Lynn to go, but she'd be back next Friday for her holidays. I wished that were now.

Once they had left, I wished they hadn't. Wished

Lynn had stayed. The house felt so empty, just me and Agatha. Already she was in her rocking chair, surveying the room with smug satisfaction. She announced, "Tomorrow this place gets a good cleaning!"

I didn't think it looked so bad and said so. Then I stripped Lynn's bedding, lugged the cot upstairs and went to bed, even though it was only seven. I had to listen to the flying squirrels for hours.

CHAPTER

TWENTY-SEVEN

Even though I didn't sleep very well, I was awake before Agatha. I got dressed, grabbed four cookies, a piece of cheese and an apple, and climbed down to my cave. I hadn't been here for over a week. Leaves and twigs had blown in. I threw them up the bank, then brushed small animal tracks out of the dirt and sat down.

The view from here looked new again. The island lay to my right at a different angle. Seemed larger. I could only see one tree, not the two I can see from directly in front.

Well, Grace Kelly, what do you have to say for yourself?

I'm sorry, Jessica. I didn't know you'd be so upset.

Well, you should have known!

I should have discussed my plans with you, so you wouldn't be surprised reading them in a newspaper.

I looked like an absolute fool! And you saw how Lynn behaved—trying to make me feel better.

She's a good friend.

Yes, she is! Better than you!

You have every reason to be mad at me, Jessica.

I sure do! And I don't need your permission! Giving up films! Marrying that—toad!

Grace Kelly laughs. Certainly I'm more beautiful than he is, but he is a prince. He's wealthy and—exciting.

Aren't movies exciting? Isn't Gary Cooper or Cary Grant? Aren't you wealthy? Hollywood's morally corrupted you! What did you do—fall in love?

You don't need to sneer, Jessica. Not so long ago you called falling in love romantic.

Don't rub it in. You could get married without giving up movies. I don't mind if you get married— if you must. But movies—why?

There, there, my dear. Don't be so upset. Here,

use my hankie, it's clean. She tries to pat my shoulder, but I pull away.

Don't "my dear" me! And don't give me your hankie! Your damn hankie! Just tell me why? You have to tell me what I need to know!

I'm an old-fashioned girl, I guess. She laughs, then turns serious again when I glare. Women give up their careers for the men they love. So they can stay home and look after them. My mother did. Your mother did. She only works now because she has to.

I'd never give up a career in movies. Anyway, I'm never getting married!

Don't say anything rash. You might regret it.

Now you sound like Agatha! Besides, married women can work if they want to.

Well, I don't want to any more. I want to be looked after—and by a prince.

You'll give up your career and marry him and he'll get sick and die.

No, he won't.

Yes, he will.

No, he won't. He's not your father.

Oh, shut up! You can't talk about my father any more! If you're going to be that way about it, go marry your prince! But I'm not coming to your wedding!

Oh, Jessica, that hurts! I really wanted you to be a bridesmaid.

Tough.

Maybe you'll change your mind?

Never. This is good-bye, Grace Kelly. Good-bye forever! And I've got my own hankie!

I didn't really. Didn't even have a tissue. I rubbed the tears with the back of my hands and sniffed. Loudly. Didn't matter. Wasn't anyone to hear.

When my father was sick and the maid or Mum was looking after him, I'd go outside so I wouldn't have to hear—to hear—to hear—Go away! Leave me alone!

He shouted at anyone. Lots of times at me. So I would go away outside—like now, dig in the dirt, like now—I planted sticks and twigs and flowers I picked to make gardens—but the next day they'd have fallen over or wilted—I was too young then to know plants need roots to grow—

After a while I ate the cookies. Then the apple, alternating it with bites of cheese. So I don't have Grace Kelly any more. I do have Agatha—and the Filly. Harv—ugh. Mum—and Lynn when I get home. My other friends. My aunts and uncles. But they're in Vancouver. I wish Lynn hadn't had to leave. We'd been having fun—until Grace Kelly ruined it.

At the Dollarton shack, Scott and Pete came to stay for a week. We made a fort and shot Scott's BB gun at a tin can, and we made houseboats out of Popsicle sticks, with string for railings and real curtains at the windows. Scott didn't make curtains, but Pete and I did. And at high tide we jumped off the porch into the water. That made the shack a real houseboat. Mum rented a rowboat and taught us how to row, and we fished off the pier. Once I hooked an orange starfish. Scott said my line was too far down.

This is how I felt when they left, like I had no friends in the world and nothing to do. I climbed my cedar tree and sat in it nearly all day.

I guess this cave is my Ontario cedar tree.

Thinking that surprised me that the lake hadn't changed into the ocean, that these birches and pines weren't cedar and alder. I sniffed for a whiff of salt air—but got warming lake and earth. A squirrel chittered above me and I looked up. Sun on the topside of branches, dappled underneath. A piece of birch bark bobbed at the edge of the lake. I picked it up—Lynn's writing, faded from water and sun—Marlon I love you. I ached with missing her.

At least Scott and Pete and I didn't kiss.

Lynn was right, it was just practising—I think. Though I don't know how you can practise something like that. You don't even practise putting on make-up. You either do it or you don't. Like you don't practise having your period. These things happen and they're there. I guess Lynn didn't get hers again—she would have said. She didn't talk about the kissing either—

I'll wait until I'm fifteen to think about kissing.

I hope Scott and Pete don't grow into teenagers like Harv. Maybe I'll write them a letter.

I re-launched the piece of bark, watched it bobble down the lake. After a bit I grew tired of sitting and thinking and feeling sad and I had nothing more to eat. Besides, it was getting hot. I picked up my apple core and trudged into the cottage. Agatha was sweeping the floor. She looked up with a smile. "Hello."

"Agatha," I blurted, "do you ever hate it when people leave? Do you ever get—lonely?"

"Indeed." She backed to a chair and sat down, her broom upright before her. "It is also quite possible to be lonely in a crowd. In fact, some say loneliness is the human condition. And transition, change—from having your friend to not having your friend—well, life is all change.

215

What one must do is put one's house in order."

Sounded as if she were quoting. "Is that Emily Dickinson?"

"No, it is strictly Agatha Adams. And it's what we will do today. Cleaning makes a good transition. It accomplishes something as well as keeps one busy." She pushed herself out of the chair. "When I have finished sweeping it, you will wash the floor. I will do the washing up. You of course will see to the kindling, the lamp chimneys and the outhouse. I will tidy. Then perhaps"— her eyes sparkled a smile, "this afternoon you will show me how you make salt-water taffy?"

I felt teary and smiley together. "Okay," I said.

And that's what we did. It took the whole day. I only went for a short swim to get the taffy-stickiness off. And by evening I felt much better.

CHAPTER

TWENTY-EIGHT

Next Friday I waited in the clearing for Mum to bump down the dirt track from the road. Twilight, and the shadows were long. From here, the week behind had gone so fast I couldn't think what I'd done, though on Monday it had stretched ahead like an empty horizon. I'd just hung around, reading, swimming, talking to Agatha. Keeping Grace Kelly out of my head. Whenever she got in wanting a conversation, I told her to go away. As the week wore on, I'd missed Lynn more and more. I wished I hadn't been so upset or had pretended not to be, for Lynn's sake. I tried three times to write her a letter, but each time my mind went as blank as the paper. I didn't know what to say except, sorry.

Sometimes, unexpectedly, all week, a heavy sadness came up in me. I felt like crying, but I didn't have any tears. If I stayed very still, and very quiet, eventually it went away.

One day when Agatha and I were both in the lake, facing the cottage next door, I asked her if they'd had cocktail parties, and had they invited her? "Yes," she replied. "They were very advanced." Her sniff indicated she didn't think advanced was necessarily good. And, "Yes, they had a piano." I was shivery that I'd known those things—felt them—in the house.

Agatha also told me about a tragedy around the bay—before the Great War. Her time really is divided into before the Great War and before the Last War. I wonder why the Boer War doesn't count, since that one killed her fiancé. Maybe it was too long ago.

Anyway, Agatha said a man had murdered his wife and child with an axe. It had been weeks before anyone found the bodies; they were smelly and decomposed, and no one had ever found him. Agatha said he probably went to the War.

This story was better than the last part of *Amarylis*—when the little girl grew up, she and John did get married—with too much boring description—and they had two children whom they—stupidly—called John and Amarylis. That was all that happened. Probably they're still admiring flowers and keeping clean.

The Studebaker engine! I leapt up, watched Mum bump into sight. I had the door open before she turned off the ignition. She looked so tired—circles under her eyes, a new line down each cheek. My heart panged.

If my father were alive, Mum wouldn't have to work. She could have been here with us all these weeks, and she wouldn't look tired. But then my father would look tired—

I gave her a big hug and took her suitcase. Heavier than usual. "You don't have to leave on Sunday," I announced. "Not for two weeks!"

Mum laughed and squeezed my shoulders. "I won't believe it until I'm still here Monday morning."

Monday morning she was sitting by the lake, reading. I asked, "Now do you believe it?"

"What?"

"That you're on holidays."

Mum stuck her finger in her book and considered. "I'm getting there," she said finally, smiling.

It was a joke from Dollarton; I could ask Mum every day if now she believed, and every day she would consider and finally answer, "I'm getting there." Except on the last day. Then she'd say, "Yes, and they're over." Now I never ask on that day.

"Mum?" I leaned on the back of her chair. "Could we please go to Emsdale? Agatha says it's not far."

"Emsdale?" She twisted her neck to contemplate me.

"Where my father grew up. You know."

"Certainly I know. I'm just surprised. It's so—out of the blue."

Not for me. I've been thinking about it for weeks. But I didn't say that.

She reached up and patted my hand, then flipped open her book. "Certainly we can go."

"Today?"

She laughed. "All right. This afternoon."

It's a good thing Mum thinks driving is a way of having a holiday.

At lunch Mum asked Agatha if she wanted to come. I really had to be an actress to not show my disappointment when she said yes. I didn't want to hurt her feelings but I wanted just Mum and me to go. Then I remembered that Mary grew up in Emsdale too, so of course Agatha would want to go.

I rode my horse in the back seat for over an hour before we got there. Agatha's not far is farther than my not far. I jumped the Little East River three times. Emsdale is exactly my sort of town. The highway doesn't even change into a street. But it isn't much of a highway to begin with. Houses with picket fences and large shady trees on both sides, a gas station, a corner store—

Everyone would have had horses here then—

My father riding bareback to the store like the boy in *Shane*—

Can I have a ride, Robert?

Okay, Jessica, but you're pretty small. You have to hold on to me—

Would he have liked me when he was a boy?

—a spire through some trees. "Bet that's it!" I shouted.

Mum stopped the car in front of a white frame church. It was long and narrow with a belfry and spire and had a white picket fence to the side. A neatly kept gravel path ran from the road to the front entrance. Under a tree, a sign in front proclaimed: St. Mark's Anglican Church. "I guess they're still using it," Mum observed.

"Of course! It's not old as churches go. Only"— Agatha snorted — "as old as I!"

"But you're not a church," I pointed out. "Can we go in?" I got out of the car and walked along the side path to the five shallow steps.

My father walked up these steps to this door. Just like this, putting his feet right here. So did his parents, and Mary. A real family. Every Sunday for years. Sudden goose-bumps on my arms. I rubbed them.

Mum and Agatha caught up with me. I twisted and pulled the ring handle, but the door was locked. We walked down again and followed the gravel along the side. Two large windows, mainly yellow and white diamonds, but stained glass pictures above.

Scrunching on the gravel. We all turned: a tall man with reddish hair, in work pants and a tartan shirt with rolled-up sleeves. "May I help you?" he offered.

Mum said, "We'd like to look around. Is that all right?"

"Certainly. I'd be glad to show you what I can. We don't get many visitors."

Mum sounded a little embarrassed. I glanced at her. Her face was flushed. "My late husband's father was minister here in the eighteen-nineties. He died here in 1898. My daughter wants to see where her father lived as a boy. Crawford is our name—"

"Oh, Reverend Crawford!" The man looked delighted. "Are you his widow, Ma'am?" This to Agatha.

"Certainly not!" she snapped. "I'm far too young!"

The man flustered. I nearly giggled, though I felt sorry for him. Maybe he had trouble at tea parties, too. "Pardon me, Ma'am, that was inexcusable. Of course, you're far too young. I wasn't thinking."

Agatha was somewhat mollified. "I am Miss Adams. The daughter of the Reverend was my good friend. Unfortunately she died in 1919. In Vancouver. The family went west before the Great War."

I didn't think Agatha had to be saying all this, but the man seemed interested.

"They moved from Emsdale when the Reverend died? I don't know what the records are of the family—I've only been here a few months. My name's Griggs. I'm the latest minister." He smiled as he shook our hands. A kind looking man, and young, for a minister. He wasn't wearing a minister's collar either. I would have guessed he was a gardener.

I fell into step with him, ahead of Mum and Agatha. "Where would they have lived?"

"In the old rectory. It burned down twenty years ago. It was over there." He pointed to the other side of the church. "They built the new one—where I'm living—right there." An ordi-

223

nary box of a house, not half so interesting as the tall cream-coloured one across the road with wooden curlicues under the eaves and lace curtains. Maybe the old rectory had been like that.

Reverend Griggs offered Agatha his arm to climb the church steps. That really mollified her. On the porch he took out a ring of keys, selected one, fit it in the lock. "The church stood open for years, shame to have to lock it, but the vandalism now—"

The door swung open. I was first inside. A smell of dusty wood and wax and flowers.

Mum and I don't go to church much. Mum says she's allergic to the flowers. She certainly can sneeze—that's embarrassing in a church. When the flowers from my father's funeral were delivered to our house, Mum put them outside on the sundeck.

He would have gone to this church when he was my age—with his father giving the sermon and shaking hands afterwards—what would that have been like?

I walked up the centre aisle towards the altar and stained glass windows. The buzz of voices wafted after me. Sunlight streamed in from the western windows, goldening the dark wood of the pews, the altar railing, the large brass cross. I slipped into the second pew.

He might have sat here between his mother and Mary—or suppose he sang in the choir? Had he liked to sing? Had he ever been bad? Would his father have turned around and frowned?

I felt sad and sort of—empty. If Mum didn't know, or Agatha, then I'd never find out. It was so long ago—

Anyway, he would have been eleven when his father died—when they moved to Toronto—younger than me now—as old as I was when we moved to Toronto—

That made me smile. He might have felt how I felt last year.

Did you feel scared and excited? Did you worry about making friends? Did you feel homesick? Did you miss your father?

I walked back to the grown-ups. "If he died here, is he buried here? In Emsdale?" I asked Reverend Griggs and Mum. I couldn't call him my grandfather. He felt too shadowy, unreal. My father's father. Anyway, I don't know anything about grandparents. Agatha would be the closest and she isn't one. She's just—Agatha. Looking tired; she had missed her afternoon read.

"Yes," said Reverend Griggs. "The cemetery's just up the hill. Would you like to look?"

He led the way out of the church, locking the door behind us. Mum helped Agatha on the steps. The heat pressed down and beat up from the gravel; the church had been cool.

We all climbed into the car and Mum drove two blocks then turned off the main road at the Reverend's directions. We bumped up a hill. To the right was a fenced meadow with gravestones. I got out; the others followed more slowly. The grass looked like short sunburned hay. It was so peaceful, no houses nearby. A real country cemetery. My father is buried in a huge park-like green grass place in the centre of Vancouver.

Reverend Griggs unlocked the padlock on the gate and we all went in. "Now, let's see if we can find your grandfather," he said to me. "One thing, he won't have gone any place." He laughed. I liked him a lot.

There weren't many graves, maybe twenty, and the headstones were all weathered grey.

"Now, let's see," he repeated. I wandered around reading the gravestones with him while Mum waited with Agatha. "Here we are." He stopped in front of a white-grey headstone with a cross on top. I read the black inscription.

THE REVEREND

ANTHONY WILLIAM CRAWFORD

1837-1898

"HE LEADETH ME..."

Shivery again, in spite of the heat. I hugged

myself—1837 was such a long time ago. If he were still alive he'd be one hundred eighteen. Grandfather, I tried in my head. Felt silly to say that to a tombstone.

My father would have been at his father's funeral, just like me at mine. Did they have pallbearers too? Did they sing "Onward Christian Soldiers"? Did he cry?

Mum was saying to Agatha, to Reverend Griggs, "Robert never talked much about his father. I have little to tell Jess—"

I caught her looking significantly at me. She smiled. It's okay, Mum, I smiled back.

"Mary said her father was stern, but just—" Agatha began.

"Oh—he was a real Victorian, then," the Reverend observed with a laugh. "Even born the year she became queen."

"Oh, yes!" Mum laughed too. "And the year of the Family Compact."

Enough history. "What else did Mary say?" I encouraged Agatha.

She leaned on her walking stick and contemplated the grave. "There were only the two children, she and Robert, so many years apart—their parents were married in England, where her father was ordained—"

Her face loosened onto a soft old smile. "Mary

227

and I came here once, in oh-five or six—some friends had a car. She wanted to show me the rectory, and the then-minister's wife allowed us through it." Now she was talking directly to me. "It was large, as I recall, and Mary's bedroom was at the front—upstairs, of course. Robert's looked out on trees at the back. Mrs. Crawford had been the church organist. Mary remembered a harpsichord in the house as well. She hated having her mother teach her, hated having to practise—"

"Was that our harpsichord?" I interrupted to Mum. She nodded. "Too bad you sold it—" I turned back to Agatha. "What other furniture was there? An oval table? Victorian chairs?"

"I suppose so. They had that furniture in Toronto." Agatha was addressing Mum, who looked sad and uncomfortable. I changed the topic a bit.

"Did my father have to play the harpsichord, too?"

Agatha dribbled off into head-shaking. "I don't remember any more. If I ever knew. So much has happened—and I'm an old lady"— sounded as if she were reminding herself—"who cannot stand the heat. If you want to be longer, Eleanor, I'll wait in the car."

I watched her shuffle across the grass, escorted by Mum and the Reverend. I heard him say, "I can look through the church records and write you—?"

"That's kind," Mum replied. "Any information would be a legacy for Jessica—" They were nearly at the car.

I turned back to the headstone, re-read the inscription. Would you have liked me? Would you have been stern but just with me? Did my father like you? Did he like me?

On the way home, Agatha had a cat nap. I wished I could have one, too. I felt deep and heavy. Not sad, just—deep. And heavy. Maybe if anyone jostled me, I could feel sad. I sat very still and wondered how my father got from this church to a hero in the war to tickling me in my bedroom? To being sick in the hospital? Outside in his dressing gown?

If Mum and I had been alone and I'd been in the front seat, I would have asked her. And asked how he died. Even if she sighed and frowned. But Agatha could wake up any minute, and I was in the back seat.

I leaned forward and put my arms on the back of the driver's seat. "Mum?"

"Mmm?" Thinking thoughts, too.

"Thanks for taking me."

"You're welcome. It was a good idea."

I leaned back and made myself think about how I'd ride the Filly along this stretch of road. It had a straight grassy verge and we could gallop, gallop, gallop—

My father is thundering along beside me on a large black stallion, waving his sword from the war over his head. Even though the Filly's smaller than his horse, she can keep up with him. My father turns to me. His strong teeth glint handsomely as he laughs, his blond hair streams like golden fire.

What a fine rider you are, Jessica!

Thank you, Father. You taught me well. And thank you for buying the Filly for me.

You're most welcome. Only the very best little mare for you! You're a daughter to be proud of!

I grin at him. We slow our horses to a trot, preparing to ford this little stream. I'm proud to be your daughter, Father!

CHAPTER

TWENTY-NINE

I'm lying in bed—a funny sort of bed with bars—
a crib. I look for someone to tell I'm too big to be
in a crib—there's Mum. She's standing on a grassy
hill. Her back's turned to me. Her shoulders are
slumped and her head's down; her hands hang
loose by her sides. I yell but she doesn't hear me.
I yell again. Again. I'm opening my mouth to yell
louder but the head of the bed is a tombstone
and the crib sides are solid grave walls. Dirt's
falling on top of me. I struggle to sit up, yelling
for Mum. No sound comes out. Hands are holding
me down—bony hands—dead hands. Now faces
are laughing at me—not faces, skulls—thick lipstick on the bones around their teeth. The hands

move. I scream. Can't make a sound. Mum can't hear. She doesn't turn, she doesn't see—she won't save me—these bony, clattering fingers are just about to grab me—

I'm drenched in sweat, but shivering. My heart's thudding and I can barely catch my breath—

Stars through the veranda screen. A dream, I tell myself. Still, I tilt my head, expecting to see a tombstone behind me—

Such a vivid dream—I want to stick my sweaty feet out but I'm too scared—skeletons that tickle—scared to move. I want to run to Mum, but it's too dark, too far, I'm too scared. I want to call for her but what if she doesn't hear? She wouldn't hear me without Agatha hearing—what if Agatha's shocked into heart failure? Anyway, I want Mum, not Agatha. I start to cry, I can't move, have to be quiet, can't let anyone know—I'm helpless—

"I've had my supper and had my supper and HAD my supper and all—"

I cry even harder, have to fight with my sobs to keep them quiet. Winnie-the-Pooh's left me too, Grace Kelly's asking why wouldn't you be alone? Now I am alone and I don't want to be—might as well be dead—maybe I am—

You know you're not, Jessica.

Oh, Grace Kelly! I might as well be.

232

Feeling sorry for yourself. She sniffs like Agatha. Go upstairs and get into bed with your Mum.

I can't. It's too dark.

You've never been scared of the dark before.

Yes, I have. Anyway, I am now.

You know it was just a dream.

Yes, Grace Kelly.

Everyone has them.

Yes, Grace Kelly. But this was an awful one!

You visited a grave yesterday. That's maybe why you dreamt about—

Don't say it, Grace Kelly! It's too scary! I roll over and put my head under the pillow. But—maybe.

Would you like to read? You have your flashlight.

No, I don't think so.

If Winnie-the-Pooh doesn't help, try Emily Dickinson. Plump up the pillow, roll onto your side, and recite her.

Well—okay. I get the pillow and blankets comfortable, then I whisper, *After great pain a formal feeling comes—*

The nerves sit ceremonious like tombs—Oh, thanks a lot, Grace Kelly!

We both laugh, although I'm shuddering.

In a minute I recite the one I learned at school—

There is no frigate like a book

To take us lands away—and I think about school, what it will be like this year in Grade Eight—will Lynn still suck her thumb?—might she get lipstick on it?—the skulls had lipstick—

I shudder and moan, then roll over and ride the Filly to school the long way around and everyone admires her and envies me for having her—

I must have fallen asleep, because it's morning. It's not true that dreams are never as scary in the day as they are at night. It's just that daylight lets you see around them better.

CHAPTER

THIRTY

"You poor dear! What a dreadful dream," Mum said when I told her and Agatha at breakfast. "You could have called me."

"I didn't think you'd hear."

"There's a point to sleeping inside like most people," Agatha sniffed. "When you need someone, someone's there."

I ignored that. When I had slept inside because of the storm, it hadn't been any comfort. Of course, I hadn't called out then, either.

"My window's right over the veranda—and it's open," Mum added. "I would have heard you."

"Oh." I hadn't thought of that. "Well." I shrugged, continued eating my toast. "Mum,"

I said, when she'd poured her second cup of coffee, "I'd like to go riding today—will you drive me? Please?"

"Why not take the bus as you have been?"

"I'm tired of the bus."

"Take the bus down and I'll pick you up." Mum had on her pleasant, reasonable tone.

"Ohhh." I snapped my tongue on the roof of my mouth. "I really want you to drive me. Please." I didn't want to go riding as much as I wanted to ask Mum about my father—and driving to the stable was the only place I could think of that Agatha wouldn't want to come.

"All right," Mum finally agreed. "But we'll go before it gets too hot."

I changed my shorts for my jeans and shoved the money in my pocket. While we walked up the path to the car, my stomach started to tickle so much I wondered if I was getting sick. Then the buzzing started—not just a thousand bees, but a thousand beehives. I was stinging and gasping with it all.

Stop it, I told myself. All you have to do is say: Mum, please tell me what my father died of. As Mum started the car I practised in my head: Mum, please—

Couldn't say it here, in the clearing. Agatha might come up the path and wonder why we hadn't left. Though she never comes up the path except to get in the car—

On the road I'd say it. Mum would pull over to the side and tell me. What he died of that was lingering and why she hadn't told me before and why she wasn't mad when he—tickled me at night—

What if Mum gets upset? What if she says I'm too young? What if she gets the scary look on her face—

When we went to California after my father died, I was playing in the sand and I looked up at Mum sitting on a rock and she looked so sad and tired and scared I wanted to throw myself at her and hug her to make that look go away. But I couldn't. I don't know why. I just turned back to the hole I was digging and dug it and dug it and dug it until I forgot.

I'd hate to make Mum look like that again. Have her maybe cry. But still, I need to know—

Mum, please tell me, Mum please—battered in my throat, growing larger and larger until it got stuck there and I almost gagged, like with a mouthful of tinned peas, the more I chew the bigger it grows.

Then Mum turned off the road up the hill to the stable. I didn't know we were so close—couldn't ask her here—Harv or Bud would stare.

And now did I have to go riding? I hadn't even thought of Harv—what if he got back at me for last time? Now my stomach really closed up so the tickles were squeezed into a smaller space. I could hardly breathe. What was worse, to ask Mum or face Harv? I practically burst with wanting Lynn here. Why did I always have to do things alone? Maybe we could just drive on. But Mum had stopped the car and I couldn't think how to explain about Harv. Oh, well, I could forget about the question for a while. Except I still had a sour taste in my mouth.

"I'll come back for you in about an hour," Mum said.

"No! Wait for me! Please?"

She looked surprised. I shrugged my shoulders and my eyebrows. Usually I don't want her to wait. "I didn't bring a book—is there a reason you want me to wait?"

"Well—"

"Are you okay, Jess?" Mum had a slight frown.

"Yes."

"Is the dream haunting you?"

"No. I'm fine." Except for a mouthful of stuck questions. And Harv. "See you later."

I waved and walked a few paces towards the stable, turned and waved again. Mum was still puzzling after me, through the windshield. Mum, please tell—I almost went back and asked her. But I was too close to the stable.

Bud and Harv were right inside the door, talking. I waited a minute, then said hi to Bud. I ignored Harv.

"Oh—hi." He had a toothpick in his mouth.

"Can I ride the Filly, please?"

"I dunno. She's a handful." Bud didn't look exactly pleased to see me. Or maybe to be interrupted. Maybe he was bawling Harv out—I hoped.

"I've ridden her. She's good as gold with me."

He turned his toothpick around with his lips, looked over to the Filly, back outside the door. He shrugged.

"Thanks." I walked up to her, patted her nose. She blew through her nostrils at me. Velvet Gold?

"You go with her, Harv."

Oh no! I whirled back to Bud. "I can go alone."

He shook his head. "Stable policy. No one goes out alone. Too dangerous."

"I have before," I said, without thinking.

Bud glared at Harv. Harv glared at me. "When?" Bud asked me, Harv.

Harv narrowed his glare into a squint at me. I backtracked. "Well, I wasn't quite alone—"

Bud spat out his toothpick, glared some more

239

at Harv. "It's not happenin' again, Harv, er yer fired. Now she takes Paint and you take the Filly—"

"No!" I almost shrieked. "I have to ride her! Please! You just said I could!"

"No, I didn't." Bud rolled his eyes and clicked his tongue, but he shrugged his shoulders okay again. Dames, did I hear him mutter? All horse crazy? Harv sneered with him and glared at me, then went to get the tack.

"See what ya did?" Harv said when we were in the woods. "Nearly got me fired. Ya watch it."

"I did not! How was I to know?" My tone was indignant, but I also felt confused. I hadn't, had I?

I patted the Filly's neck. I'd thought about her so much since I'd last ridden her, I'd been afraid she'd be less glorious than I remembered. She wasn't. Being on her made me less scared of Harv. What could he do on horseback? I thought maybe the Filly was pleased I, and not Harv, was riding her. But she had a large manure splotch on her right hip. "Don't you ever groom the horses?" I shouted.

"Sure," he lied, without looking back. Down the hill a way, he asked, "Where's yer girlfriend?"

"Gone home."

"Where's that?"

"Toronto."

"City girls. Pretty refined, eh? I bet ya know a lot o' things." My skin crawled at Harv's creepy tone. He halted Paint and half-turned him so he was blocking the trail.

The Filly was forced to stop, too. She resentfully pawed the ground and tossed her head. I flicked my eyes from one side to the other but the trees were too thick to barge through. Trapped. The only way out was back. My armpits prickled with sudden sweat. A fly landed on the Filly's neck but my hands were shaking too much to brush it off. I moved the rein up. The fly just moved up, too. The Filly thought I meant move, and did. But she had no room to move.

"So—get going." My voice was hoarse. I swallowed to silently clear my throat.

Harv just lounged on Paint, leering at me. "Don't ya?"

"What?" Though I knew.

"Know a lot o' things. Don't ya." He flicked out his rat-tail comb as if it were a knife. Paint seemed happy to stand there forever.

I thought, What would Lynn do? I thought of Mum waiting in the car. "Come off it! You get going or I'm going back!" I started to turn the Filly.

"Won't help. Bud's gone fer feed." His tone had a smug smile in it.

"Oh, come on! He doesn't go for feed every week—" Does he? I had the Filly nearly around, could gallop back to the stable—

"Jus' gimme one kiss and we'll get goin', though neckin's better'n ridin' any day." Leering, with a lip curl.

Now I was mad. That stopped me from being as scared. "You are so disgusting! Where do you get the nerve to think I'd kiss you! I'd die first!"

"Sure, sure." But I maybe saw a bit of surprise on his face before it sneered again? "Yer jus' playin' hard to get. When ya stop, I'll kiss ya big, baby. Like ya never been kissed before. I know yer dyin' fer it."

I couldn't believe it! Wait till I told Lynn! Now I was really mad. "I am not going to kiss you! Where do you get off thinking I want to!"

"All girls do. Especially from the city." Harv sounded so serious, so convinced. I just stared at him with my mouth open.

"Not me! Not Lynn! Not any girls I know! You are the biggest drip I have ever met! And I hate the way you talk! From now on, you keep your kissing talk and your horny talk to yourself! And if you don't get going this minute, I'm galloping back to the stable and telling Bud you never turned in that money!"

I glared at him glaring at me. Creep, I thought, and, crud, to keep my hands and knees from trembling. The Filly was getting restless. She might bolt any minute. But I couldn't take my eyes off him to soothe her.

Finally, with an enormous lip snarl, Harv hauled Paint around and started down the trail. The Filly leapt forward so closely she snapped at Paint's haunches. He kicked out, but missed. I pulled her back, patted her neck, got her more under control, then I just jellied along on top.

At the bottom stream, Harv pushed into a sudden canter. The Filly took it as a challenge and leapt ahead in three strides.

I struggled to stay aboard—You creep, trying to unseat me!—remembered the make-up woman who'd fallen off. I glanced over my shoulder: Harv's teeth clenched between parted lips. He was really racing!

I leaned low over the Filly's neck, gave her her head and squeezed my legs for encouragement. I thought she'd been going full out, but she surged up more power. I was nearly blown out of the saddle. It took me a few strides to settle into her rhythm, then my fear turned to excitement. I shortened the reins and pushed my hands forward on her neck. "*Go* girl," I yelled. "*Go* Filleeee!"

The fence drew us up half a field in front of Harv and Paint. She snorted and pranced and gave a little buck. I cantered her in slower and slower circles while they caught up. The Filly's nostrils flared and she tucked her chin into her chest as if she knew she'd won. Which she probably did. I was sure telling her she had. Even though Harv had the slower horse.

She and I led out of the meadow and along the lake shore. Harv might have been looking at me—I could feel his eyes burning through my blouse—but I never once turned around. I worried that he might overtake me, grab my arm, and throw me off, but when I worried that, I urged the Filly to trot. The only thing Harv said the whole way was, "There's another trail up there," just past the point Lynn and I had turned back. His tone was neutral, but it could have been neutral like a car revving up. He didn't talk at the stable, either. I knew he was watching me cross to the Studebaker. I put all our triumph into keeping my knees from giving way.

THIRTY-ONE

"How was your ride?" Mum asked.

I grinned. "Wonderful! Did you see the Filly?" Harv had just led her into the stable. "Isn't she grand? Isn't she glorious?"

"She is indeed." Mum has learned a bit about horses from me.

"Why don't we buy her? She'd only cost fifty dollars, I bet—well, maybe a hundred—"

"It's not the cost of the horse, it's—"

"—the cost of the up-keep," I finished with her. We both laughed, though I ached for the Filly, too.

"I'd love to buy you a horse, Jess, but we can't afford it." Mum started the car, reversed, turned, slowly inched down the hill. "Although I have a good job, I'm still paying bills from your father's illness. It will take a few more years before we're out of debt."

Debt? It took me a minute to register the word, to locate its meaning, even though I knew I knew it. Then it hit me in the stomach—*debt*. I gasped, "I didn't know we were in debt!"

I must have sounded as shocked as I felt. Mum said lightly, as if she wished she hadn't said anything, "Not to worry. It's under control." She waited for a car to pass, then turned left onto the road.

"What do you mean—it wasn't always under control?" Right this minute I wanted to face a thousand Harvs rather than this.

But Mum was saying, "Yes."

I tried to get my stomach relaxed. If I didn't, I'd throw up. "Is that why we sold all the furniture? The harpsichord?"

"Yes."

"How much debt?"

"A lot." Mum's close-the-topic tone.

I struggled against wanting to close the topic myself. It would be so easy—I could ignore it, forget it, not know. But I needed to know. Everything. "How much, Mum?" I was biting my nail.

She glanced at me, back to the road. I wished she'd stop driving, but I wanted her to keep on. "I thought we shared," I said. "I'm old enough to know." *Was I?*

Mum slowed for a curve, speeded up halfway around, as she always did. "I still owe twelve thousand dollars." Her tone flat.

"We owe." More money than I'd ever thought about. "That's three years of your salary."

"Except we have to eat. We seem to like doing that." She laughed.

I looked at my bitten nail, rubbed my thumb over it. I have never imagined thousands of dollars. If we had a winning Sweepstakes ticket—I couldn't think about it. Except I had to. "How long do you figure, then?"

"With luck, six years."

I'd be eighteen. An old teenager. Out of high school. I couldn't imagine it.

"What made us go into debt?"

"Oh—housekeepers, nurses, hospital bills. Our insurance covered some of it, and the Veterans' Act, but—very little at the end." Sounding dismissive. Or reluctant.

"Mum." I spat the question out before it stuck again. "Please tell me about my father's death."

"He had heart failure."

"You always say that."

"It's true. That's what he died of."

"Agatha said he died lingeringly. What's she mean? Why was he in the hospital so much? How come we owe so much money?"

Mum's hands tightened on the steering wheel. Her bloodstone ring winked in the sunlight. She glanced at me, back to the road, and I couldn't tell what was in her look. I didn't want to upset her, but I had to know. I tried to look reassuring. She gave me a little smile with sadness in it. But when she spoke, her tone was firm, almost matter-of-fact.

"He had an illness—a disease. Whatever it is—and no one knows what causes it—it affects the brain so the person becomes senile early."

I stared through the windshield. Ahead, the road had patterns of water across it, but I knew when we got there it would be dry. A mirage. This sounded so awful I wasn't sure I wanted to know any more. But finally we'd started—

"What's senile?" I cleared my throat.

"It means losing one's senses, not knowing who you are or where you are, not remembering what you just did or what time of day it is, not recognizing those you used to love." Mum's voice faltered.

248

"I don't want to upset you, Mum—"

"It's all right, Jess. Talking about it brings it back, but that's okay." She touched my knee. Her turn to be reassuring. But then she speeded up.

"Did he—get like that?"

She nodded.

"Not recognize me—or you?"

"At the end. Before that, for a year or two, he'd have flashes of recognition."

Once I'd taken a picture I'd drawn in school to the hospital—a house not flat on the page like little kids do, but one that had the side of the house going away into the distance. It was the first time I'd drawn a house like that and I was proud of it. I'd painted it with water-colours and put a tree with birds and squirrels beside it. Flowers in front.

"Here's a picture for you, Daddy."

He looked at it and put it down. But there wasn't a table by his chair. It fell to the floor. I picked it up and handed it to him again.

"Here's my picture, Daddy."

"House."

"Yes!" Waiting for him to say, That's a very good house, Jess.

But he rolled it up and tried to put it in his mouth. Mum took it away from him, put it on the bedside table. I guess he thought it was a cigarette.

Did I call him daddy after that?

Flashes of recognition.

I'd forgotten that, till now. I blinked. Burning tear grit in my eyes. "I remember," I said to Mum.

"It wasn't that he didn't love you—didn't love us—it's just that he couldn't. It was a disease. It's important to remember that!" Mum peered intensely through the windshield, at me, again through the windshield. I nodded.

A clearing up ahead. Mum slowed into it, turned off the ignition. Thank heaven we'd stopped. There was a sudden press of silence and heat. I rolled down the window, leaned my elbow on it.

"Why? Why did he get that?"

Mum shrugged and shook her head. "No one knows, Jess. No one knows where it comes from. There's no cure and—not much anyone can do. Maybe there will be some day."

"What's the disease called?"

Another shrug. "No one agrees. Arteriosclerosis or pre-senile dementia—"

I fiddled with the door handle. Some part of me had taken over and was asking all these questions. Another part of me was very carefully not feeling anything. "What was it like?"

She rubbed her hands on the steering wheel, round and around. Moved her foot off the gas pedal, on again. Her eyes roved this way, that way, searching. She sort of snorted. "Like having a toddler you have to watch every minute, a toddler who can't tell night from day, who can't remember when you said 'no' or when it last ate. A toddler who's growing down into a baby so he can't feed himself, clean himself—the difference is, you know a toddler will grow up. With an adult you've married, your partner—" Mum's voice was hard. She rubbed the steering wheel harder, straightened her fingers, rubbed her face. Her tone softened. "Your father always behaved like a perfect gentleman to me."

"What do you mean?" That he didn't to others?

"I mean he never hit me." She sounded proud. I felt proud with her, though it felt funny to feel proud of that, until—

"But I saw him hit you!" I blurted. "I got out of bed and was crossing the top of the stairs to the bathroom and he had his coat and hat on. You came up behind him and reached for his collar and he whacked his arm back and hit you." My nose filled with tears. I hadn't known I'd seen that until now. "I didn't know what to do. I just went back to bed." And wet it.

"But that wasn't a real hit," Mum explained to

someone on the hood of the car. "It was more a push because I was taking his coat off. He couldn go out. He thought it was morning and time to go to work, but it was the middle of the night. And he hadn't worked for at least a year."

"Looked like a real hit to me. Hurt you. You shoulders slumped down and you put your hand to your face like the world was ending." Five or six again, looking down from the landing in my nightie. My stomach pinched in terror. Rising up to my throat even now. Why had the part of me that wasn't feeling anything left?

Mum reached over and took my hand. I tried to stop its trembling for her. "Oh, Jess. I didn' know you saw that. I'm so sorry. I tried to protect you the best I could. I tried to keep him away from you—"

"He came into my bedroom and pulled my covers off and tickled me and you just led him out. I thought you should get mad at him for doing that. For scaring me."

Tears in her eyes. She sighed out hugely through loose-parted lips and shrugged helplessly. Now she looked as old as Agatha and I was really scared. "Mum! It's okay! We don't have to talk about it! Ever!"

She squeezed my hand, sighed again, but when

she spoke her voice was Mum's. "It was a hard time, Jess, for all of us. It's hard to talk about it without feeling the pain. That night? There wasn't any point in being mad with him. He wouldn't have understood. I got him out right away, before—"

She glanced at me. I couldn't look at her, watched a fly crawl over the windshield. "I hope I did. I did, didn't I?" I nodded. What else to do?

"He went to the hospital then. I knew he had to go, for your sake. I thought you were asleep. Hoped you didn't know." She rubbed the hand that wasn't holding mine over her eyes, then looking at me searchingly. "Jess? Did he ever—hurt you? Touch you? Hit you—?"

I shrugged. "I don't know. That's all I remember." I felt flat now and tired and prickly with held-back sobs. But Mum looked as if she felt the same way. "It must have been awful for you," I said. I'd never thought about how it was for her before.

"It was awful for everyone. You, me, him—Jess, if you remember anything more, will you tell me? It's not good to keep memories locked away. They can fester, like sores."

Mum was looking at me seriously, intently, but the look had question hooks. She'd sent him to the hospital, for my sake? I twirled the knob around on the window handle. "Yes," I said finally. "But I don't remember anything."

"If you do."

"If I do." But I don't want to remember anything—isn't this enough? "Did you know from when he got it—when was that?—"

"Before you went to kindergarten—you were four. But he functioned pretty well for a while, so no one knew."

"—that he'd never get better?"

"Yes." The look on Mum's face in California—

I threw myself at her and hugged her hard, crying. "I'm so sorry! I wish I'd been more help! I would be now!"

She patted my back, crying too. "You were a great delight and comfort to me. And to him, until—"

He forgot who I was, I finished for myself. We were silent for a while, sniffing quietly. I could hear Mum's heart beating. Then my voice was saying, "The last time I saw him before he died, he was lying in bed under a white counterpane. I said, 'Hello.' He turned his head from the window and said, 'Hello' too—maybe he said, 'Hello.' There were pocketbooks on the bedside table and I thought he was getting better because he was reading. That nurse didn't remember my

254

name. She said, like they did in the hospital, 'Here's Jocelyn to see you, Mr. Crawford.'"

"Yes. That was the day before he died. Those were my books. I sat up with him at night." Mum's chin rested on the top of my head. She was stroking my hair. I had my face buried in her chest.

"Did you get any sleep?"

"Not much, the last months."

"Was it better when he was in hospital?"

"Easier at home, and better for you, but every time he saw me, he wanted to be home—"

"Is that why you brought him home?"

"Yes." Mum's voice was intense. I could feel her heart speed up. "I had to, for my own conscience. But I've asked myself—was it the right thing? Especially for you. Although by then he couldn't get out of bed."

"By then I was older. I could play outside all the time, or over at Scott and Pete's."

"Yes, you did." Mum paused, then, "It was very hard on you." Sounding so sad.

"It was hard on you too, Mum." She tightened her arms around me and I patted her back.

"You must remember he had a disease, Jess. He was a fine man, a gentleman, he led a noble life, he would have been a good father, you must remember that—"

Gentleman. Ladies. I don't know. A perfect gentleman, but he did hit her, I saw him. My father. From that church to the war hero to rolling up my picture, yelling, throwing things, forgetting me, tickling me—I wish she'd told me sooner, she shouldn't not have told me—but I was too little—are there things you can't tell children? Things she still hasn't told me? I don't want to know any more.

Still—"Mum? Are there things you haven't told me?"

She rubbed her chin on my head, gently. "Not that I can think of." Pause. "Are there things you haven't told me? Asked me?"

"Not that I can think of." Well—Harv, and kissing Lynn, and Grace Kelly, but those aren't the things we mean. I don't think. "Mum?"

"Mmm?"

"Tell me a happy story about him, about be-fore—"

"About before?" She shifted and I looked up. She was staring through the windshield. Her lashes were wet, but there were no tears on her cheeks. I blinked mine. She grew a soft memory smile and looked down at me.

"One summer we drove to the Okanagan and there was a grasshopper plague. You would have been two and a half. It was too hot to roll up the windows to keep the grasshoppers out so they flew in and jumped around. They were horrendous, but you weren't scared at all. You thought it such fun, catching grasshoppers and putting them out the window. You explained it all to them first, why they couldn't be in the car. It kept you busy for hours. Except each time you jumped up to catch one, you knocked your father's hat in his eyes and he couldn't see to drive. He got pretty exasperated. Finally he took his hat off and put it on you, and there you were, a wee mite of a thing, wearing your father's hat and talking to the grasshoppers!"

I smiled into her chest through my tears. Then I sat up and looked in the glove compartment for a tissue. I took one and handed one to Mum. We both blew.

"I think I remember the grasshoppers," I said, "and I remember having picnics on the beach—"

"We had some good times." Mum sounded wistful. And some bad times, I didn't mean to think.

I felt sad and heavy and a little lighter all at once. Mainly heavy and mainly big. As if I suddenly had more room inside me.

"Mum, I'm sorry I threw the hankie in your

lap. In the limousine. I didn't mean to hurt your feelings. I just knew I wouldn't cry at the funeral."

She looked startled, then remembering. Her eyebrows and lips pulled up into a sad, semismile. "He wasn't a father for you to cry for by then. Maybe it was a blessing he died."

"That's the saddest part. He died before he died."

Mum's hands were back on the steering wheel as if she wanted to drive somewhere. She was nodding through the windshield at whoever it was on the hood. Then she turned and smiled at me. I smiled back, loving her grey hair and the lines on her face, the steady clearness of her eyes. Loving her large hands with the veins sticking out. Her bloodstone ring that my father gave her—I'd never seen it off.

"Do you think we could handle a milkshake in Dorset?" Mum asked, switching on the ignition. "We could take one home to Agatha."

"I love you, Mum," I blurted, teary in a different way. She squeezed my hand and smiled. Then she shoved the gearshift into first and stepped on the gas.

So there you are, Grace Kelly. Now you know. Now we know, Jess.

258

That's what I meant. Pretty awful, isn't it?

Yes.

I just hope your prince doesn't get this growing-down disease.

So do I. If he does, I hope I can be like your Mum.

I don't think anyone can be like my Mum. But you can try. Have you changed your mind about giving up pictures?

No.

Thought not. Well, I probably won't be talking to you much if you're not making movies—

I'll miss you.

You know what you can do about it, Grace Kelly.

Yes. But I can't.

Good-bye, Grace Kelly. I just wanted you to know.

I appreciate it, Jess. Thank you. And good-bye.

This good-bye didn't feel so bad. Of course I keep bringing her back to say good-bye to—

I leaned back hard into the car seat and stretched my arms. Aching muscles. I'd forgotten about riding the Filly. Racing Harv. I thought of telling Mum—but I could tell her later. Then I had a tense breath choke about Agatha—we'd been gone a long time—but she hadn't died so far this summer—and Mum was here now—maybe next summer we could go home to Vancouver— see Scott and Pete and Susan—go to Dollarton— maybe Lynn could come.

I sat up. "Mum?"

"Mmm?"

"Remember when we were at Dollarton and you rented the rowboat?"

"Mmhmh?"

"Why don't we rent a canoe? You used to canoe. You can teach me!"

"Hah!" Mum laughed. "Now that's an idea! We could paddle around the lake! There must be places to rent canoes here, Agatha might know! She used to canoe, she told me, maybe we can even get her into it—"

I'm riding the Filly bareback and bridleless along the lake shore. Mum and Agatha in a red canoe. Hi! I shout. Mum and Agatha paddle closer. I leap down from the Filly and leave her to graze. I know she won't go anywhere while I'm in the canoe. And she likes her new name—Velvet Steel.

I wade into the water and start swimming. Mum steers the canoe closer. When I'm along-side, Mum and Agatha put their paddles down and help me aboard with strong hands. I get them both wet, flopping in, and we all laugh. I sit

n the middle between them and they take up
heir paddles. We're swooshing through the wa-
er and I look over for Velvet—

I can't see her anywhere. I'm in a panic, have to
eap out of the canoe, swim back to shore to find
her, but then I look closer. Her head bobbing
above the water, she's swimming out to me, she
wants to come too—

I dive back in and swim my fastest crawl to
her. When I grab her mane and stroke her neck,
she calms, and her eyes stop rolling so wildly. I
get on her back and we swim alongside the
canoe, Mum and Agatha slowly paddling down
he shoreline. I'm holding Velvet's mane and
grinning—